TO CATCH A LADY
LORDS & LADIES & LOVE, BOOK 1
Published by *The Bitter End Publishing*

Copyright © 2018 -2021 by Gina Danna

Previously published a A MERRY WICKED CHRISTMAS

All rights reserved. Except for use in any review, the reproduction or utilization of this work in whole or in part in any form by any electronic, mechanical or other means, now known or hereinafter invented, including xerography, photocopying and recording, or in any information storage or retrieval system, is forbidden without the written permission of the publisher.

This is a work of fiction.

Printed in the USA.

Cover Design and Interior Format

To Catch A Lady

Gina Danna

Acknowledgements

PHINEAS AND MARINA'S CHRISTMAS ROMANCE was a fun story to write. I couldn't have done this without the help of my editor, Louisa Cornell and critique readers Deborah Cracovia and Ann Bracken. Without their assistance, this holiday Regency story might never had seen the light of day. Thank you, ladies.

And to the beauty of the holidays and the fun of house parties during the Regency – a fun time to discover!

May all your Christmas dreams come true!

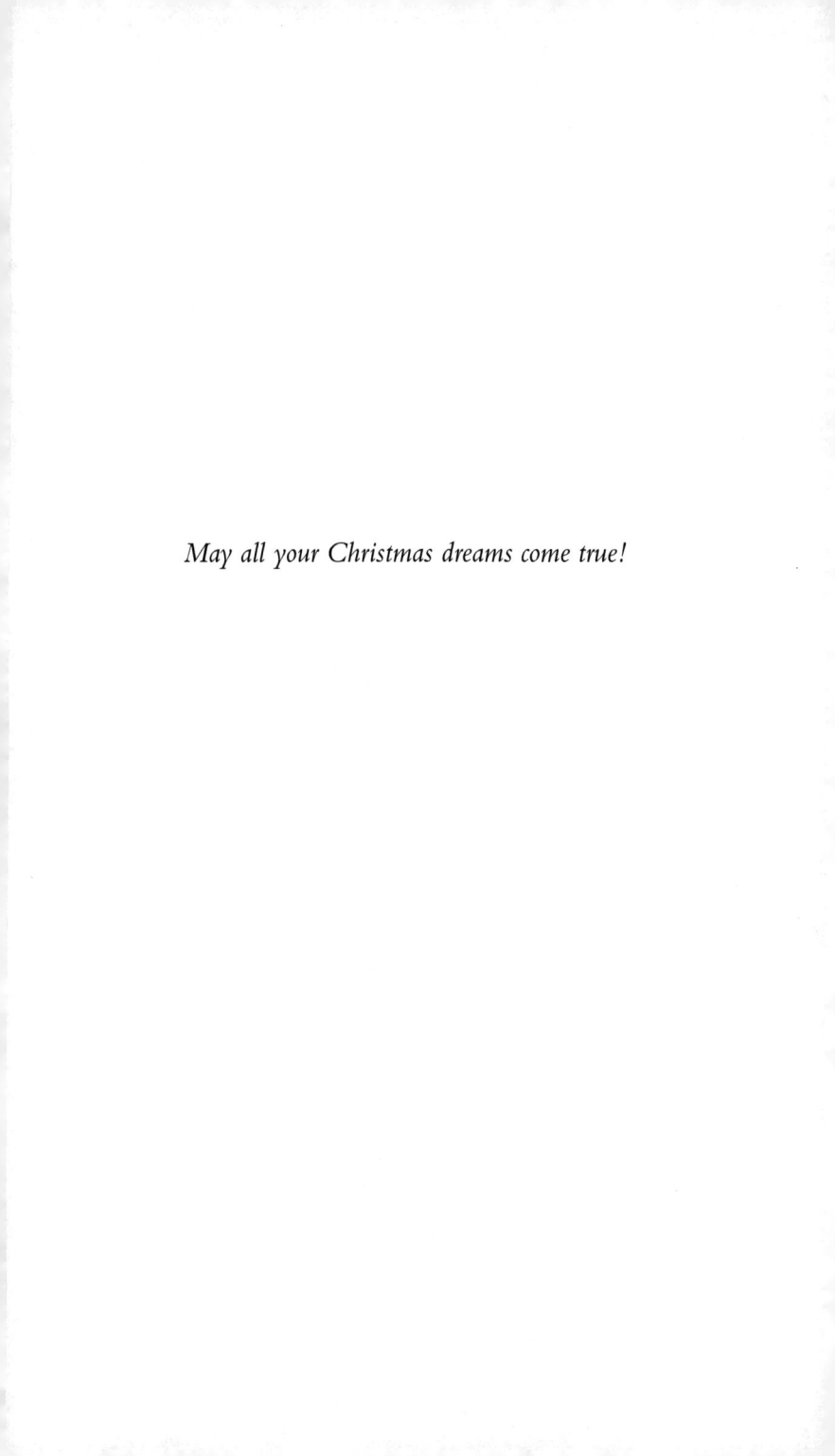

Chapter One

London
December 1815

"MARINA, MARINA, DID YOU SEE? It's snowing!"

Lady Marina Lockhart smiled, though she didn't look up from her embroidery. Her younger cousin skidded to a stop in front of her, her skirts brushing against Marina's and almost knocked the silk thread that trailed from her needle to the floor.

"Have a care, little one," she laughed, finally glancing up. "It snows all the time in the winter."

Ruth stomped her feet. "Hasn't snowed yet this winter," she huffed. But her angered face soon changed to an excited one. "That means the holiday house party will be a success!"

Marina bit her bottom lip, trying to finish the last stitch of the rose on the handkerchief, before getting up. The piece didn't need to be done before they left, but she wanted it to be. Perhaps, it would hold off the future that lay before her. She'd never felt so weak in all her living days. Told this was her last social engagement before the Season started next year, she'd also been informed her hand had been offered for already. She just prayed her papa was wrong…

"Please, Marina! We have to finish packing! You'll want to take that new dress. The marquis would never deny an opportunity to ask about you if you wear it. It's too beautiful to ignore!"

Marina put her work down and smiled at her cousin. Ruth was too young to know how the world turned, she thought. "The marquis is throwing this party for the men to go hunting and to appease his sister, who also will be coming out next spring. I doubt we will see *him*."

Ruth leaned forward and whispered in a conspiratorial tone, "Everyone knows he needs a wife, too." Then she winked at her.

Surprised, Marina could only shake her head and laugh. If only he did need one as badly as she needed a husband. He was very handsome, rich and not a scoundrel, or so she had overheard from her father. But if the marquis was such a fine catch, why hadn't her papa pursued him for her husband? Why leave her with that overweight boar, Lord Goodwood? She shut her eyes. She might as well go to the party and enjoy the end of her freedom. Rumor had it, Lord Goodwood's first wife had died from boredom…

Leaning low and forward, Phineas Huntington, the Marquis of Rockford, gave his stallion a slight nudge of his heels to goad the equine faster as they raced through the woods. They were supposed to be part of the fox hunt, but he wasn't in the mood to kill an innocent animal today. The fox he had raised from a kit was out here. She still came to the garden house, where he liked to go for a personal reprieve from the demands his position dumped on him. Petunia, he called her, still nibbled out of his hand and actually got him out of his chair to play. Even now, he laughed at all her humorous antics, jumping like a rabbit but higher and in a circular way, her fuzzy tail flapping like the wild feathered dust wand the maids used.

Even now, as he raced through the woods, he was baiting her to find him and track him and Star back to the estate, the back way, away from the hunt. Pushing the stallion faster still, he caught a glimpse of red, streaming through the trees and evergreens and it made him smile. She'd seen him.

He steered the horse back towards his garden house, slowing by the time he arrived, threw his leg over the saddle and slid to the ground, barely hitting it before a red lightning bolt jolted through the sky and into his chest. He fell back, laughing as the fox barked at him in a chirping tone. She jumped off and bounced about. One thing about this animal that made him smile was her apparent pleasure at being with him, a man. A man who was a hunter, the type of species that went after creatures like her. But she had changed him.

Of course, he was planning a house party with men who intended to hunt while the ladies did what ladies did. So, with a certain sense of regret, he'd take the men on a chase. But his little Petunia would be safe. Even now, he tested her intelligence, surprising himself at how quickly this little rascal applied what was taught. His latest venture was teaching her how to hide, something he'd bet instinctively she knew, but he wanted more. He'd built a tunnel under his garden house and placed a burrow inside, lined with straw and a touch of feathers and pine, a place well hidden and secluded. Now, teaching her to retreat there, though, was the challenge and one he took on with gusto, for he'd not have her harmed, not even by accident!

Suddenly, she stopped, mid-action, her nose high, sniffing, then a direct turn to her right. In another second, she slithered down the tunnel and out of sight, without his entreaties. With a frown, Phineas looked in the direction she'd turned and found a horse and rider slowly riding up. It was his sister, Anne. Phineas stood, straightened his trousers and jacket and strode to meet her.

"I knew I'd find you here," she said, dropping her reins and waiting for him to help her dismount off the sidesaddle.

He snorted as he lifted her lithe form and lowered her to the ground. "I like the peace here." He narrowed his gaze. "And not to be disturbed, unless it is fire or the whole of London falling." But her grin made him laugh.

"Of course, Regent before family. I do so beg your pardon," she mimicked a curtsy. Lifting her brows, she continued, "I see your friend has learned to hide when others come close. As sweet as that animal is, I fail to understand why you play with her, but claim the sniffles whenever you see my Genevieve."

"Your pet is a cat, Anne," he replied flatly. "Cats make my eyes itch."

"Oh, horse-feathers!" She laughed. "I love you in spite of your flaws, brother." She flattened her skirt and tilted her head. "What will you do when your friends decide to shoot her? After all, you invited them to hunt."

"I did not invite them of my own free will," he stated, gathering his horse's reins. "This is for your party."

"Hardly! Single ladies do not issue invitations to gentlemen for house parties. The scandal!" She mocked an open-mouthed look of surprise.

"I am hosting this party, in hopes of finding you another candidate—"

"I have given my hand to Ewan," she started.

"No, I have not approved."

"He is your best friend!" Her expression showed how perplexed she was, but he didn't care.

"Precisely, which is why I won't give my blessing." He took her by the shoulders. "You've known Ewan most of your life. You need to see who else there is."

"I want no one else!"

"Well, throwing a tantrum does not give your argument much to stand on." He ran his fingers through his hair before shoving his hat back on. "Acting as your guardian, Anne, can be taxing."

"Oh, I see." She pursed her lips. "Well, perhaps you'll find a wife."

"No."

"Phineas," she started, lacing her free arm through the crux of his. "You know as well as I that you need to wed and continue the family name."

"Mother and father expected too much, leaving me to raise you," he sighed. "At times, my dear, you're worse than Ewan on some matters."

"Which is why, we are the perfect couple." She smiled.

Phineas growled. "You will not spend your time with Ewan during this party. And I will keep him busy, so you may enjoy yourself." He stopped and turned toward her, just as her mouth opened to protest. "No. Ewan is a friend, yes, but I believe you need to meet others, enjoy this time with your friends. It is the holidays. I expect nothing less."

She squinted in protest but then laughed. "Yes sir!"

As she prattled on about who was arriving and when, Phineas nodded but his thoughts wandered. Their mother died after Anne's birth, and the late marquis just four years ago, from a carriage accident, leaving Phineas, who had just turned an age to join the military for the uprising against Napoleon, glued to the properties and raising his sister. It was a job he wasn't ready for, but one he had no choice over.

And of course, as he remained the only heir outside a distant cousin living in the New World, he was the heir to the property and title, requiring him to marry and father the next marquis. The entire situation only made him snarl. Last thing he wanted was a woman to fill a role, like a wife.

"Look! Look! Marina, we're here!!"

Marina looked up and stared out the window. It was pitch black out. She stifled a yawn only to have her cousin gave her a push. "I apologize, but it's been a long journey inside a carriage."

Ruth's expression, though, never lost enthusiasm over her cousin's reaction. "I know, I know, but

I'm far too excited to think of sleeping! Oh!" She fell back on the seat, panting. "To think of all the opportunities before us." She grinned.

Marina chuckled. "We are here for a social gathering of friends, not to husband hunt."

Ruth's brows furrowed. "Perhaps, but if one was to present itself."

"Just how well do you know Lady Anne?"

"I met her at those dreadful dance lessons my mama sent me to three years ago, when I had the body of a medusa!"

Marina couldn't help but laugh. Girls in their early teens were gangly, not as coordinated though they tried their best. It was an awkward age, mostly because that's when boys were seen as anything other than heathens. "Well, you have grown into a beautiful young lady and ready to be seen by all. I'd wager you'll take the young men like a storm." How could she not? Ruth was not too tall to tower over any of them, with a sweet cherubic face and adorable smile. Her golden hair and sparkling blue eyes made her look angelic. And if any man ever harmed her, Marina would make him regret he'd ever been born.

Ruth's smile grew larger as she reached across and took Marina's hands in hers. "I will be second to you. You are like Persephone, a true queen, all grace and beauty."

Marina choked. "Persephone? She was stolen by Hades and forced to live in the underworld!"

"Ah, but she was the daughter of Zeus and so beautiful, Hades craved her to be his queen." She sighed with a dreamy look in her eyes.

Marina stared at her cousin hard. Queen of Hell

was not a comparison to which she aspired. "I think we need to re-think your reading choices, my dear."

Both girls broke into laughter as the carriage came to a halt. They looked at each other, immediately silent but barely able to contain more giggles. It took another second to control her enthusiasm and Marina worked fast, to be more ladylike, before the door opened. The butler gave them a blank look, but Marina knew as well as the servant did. With a grin creeping back onto her face, she stepped out of the carriage and bounded up the stairs to the country mansion with Ruth racing up right behind her.

"Marina!" Ruth whispered in a quick rushed voice. "If Aunt Clare saw us…"

Their aunt, Lady Clare Lockhart, was in the carriage behind them. Marina snorted. "You know riding in a carriage at this late in the ride, she'll be watching that chamber pot under the seat closely. She won't notice." Or so she hoped. Aunt Clare always took sick on long rides, particularly at night when on a long journey.

"Lady Ruth and Lady Marina! Behave yourselves!" Aunt Clare chimed, as if on cue.

Both girls laughed as they made it to the door but stopped, stood straight as they quieted down. Ruth reached across and took Marina's hand and squeezed. As the sound of Clare's cane and footsteps grew, the front door opened. Marina couldn't help but discern her cousin's excitement. They were at Rockford Hall and it was Christmastide. A week to relax, a week to have fun, before spending the rest of her life chained to a man who touted his title as if it were high. A man who could devour half a sideboard at any meal. She shuddered until her hand went numb from Ruth's tight grip.

"Forget that whale," her cousin hissed. "My gift to you is a week of fun and games and a chance to meet a true Prince Charming." She smiled.

Marina maintained her smile, forced as it was, and hoped this Christmas wish came true, for the reality of her life was bleak.

"Welcome to Rockford Hall, miladies."

Chapter Two

CLARE LOCKHART LOOKED AT HER two nieces and was both happy and filled with anxiety over her position as chaperone. With her brother, the Earl of Lockhart, widowed, she stepped in to guide and watch, a task she took on as if she was a knight for the king, yet taking on two young ladies by herself, it was a daunting position. If nothing else, she'd box both their ears by the end, she was sure, and correct the misguidance of their parents. Sending such young does out into the world of wolves. Seeing them bound up the stairs, as if at home with no one watching, instantly put her heart into scattered beats. Her immediate call to compose themselves was obeyed at once, before the door to this lordship's house opened. After all, if the marquis had just witnessed their mad scrabble up the stairs, he could just as quickly rescind their invitation and send them back to London.

Shaking that thought from her head, Clare stiffened her back and put more weight on herself instead of relying on her cane. With a smile, she followed the ladies in and found their hostess was on hand to greet them warmly. Anne Huntington was a beauty, she mused. Not as lovely as Marina, though perhaps more graceful in her demeanor and poise. Hard to believe she was the same age as the Lockhart girls, all of twenty, a thought that staggered the mind, for Clare was married with her first on the way at twenty. Oh, how things changed, she thought, with a swift flash of sadness. Both her husband and son had died due to consumption years ago, leaving her the aging widow. She sighed.

"Lady Lockhart, what a pleasure," Anne greeted, walking her way with the two guests, Lady Amanda Hatfield and Lady Elisa Jennings in tow.

Clare smiled with a slight bow of her head. "You as well, Lady Anne."

"Please, oh please, let us dispense with the formalities for our visit," Anne leaned close and whispered. "I fear I will err more ways than not." She pulled back and lifted her voice, adding, "This is a festive time, of close friends and family and we should act as such."

"Here, here!" a male voice resounded from the room to the right. In a moment, the owner of the voice appeared, leaning slightly against the doorframe, casually attired, perhaps too much so, Clare thought. He was sans a jacket and holding a wine glass, but as lord of the manor and at this late hour, she'd forgive his impertinence.

"Phineas, please," Anne started as she turned to her guests. "Please forgive my brother. He's had quite a day, with all the guests arriving, including those he invited." She shot him a narrow gaze over her shoulder.

The Marquis of Rockford gave her a lazy smile in return. Clare's jaw tightened when she saw her two nieces brighten at it, no doubt thinking it was toward them and not a slant at his sister. It was on that, she decided, to intervene.

"Lady Anne, it was a long journey, the type of journey they are not accustomed to, so I'm sure they'd appreciate a place to refresh themselves."

"Oh, yes, certainly. Ladies," she motioned for the maid to take them, the servants carrying their trunks directly behind them.

Clare watched them head up the stairs, talking to Lady Anne who accompanied them, before she turned toward the young lord and without hesitation, went straight to him.

"Lord Rockford, please excuse our late arrival. One of our horses went lame, thus we had a later start."

Rockford snorted as he took her hand and gave it a perfunctory kiss. He was drunk, she decided, though considering his past, she could understand why. When he said nothing and spun on his heels to return to his library, she followed.

"I wanted to offer my condolences on the loss of Lady Montberry. A tragic loss of a life so young."

Her words stopped Phineas in his tracks. Of course she would go through the ritual of sympathy over the loss of his betrothed. He breathed deeply and tried his hardest not to roll his eyes. He poured more wine into his glass and offered her a glass. She denied it with a shake of her head. Pity, he thought. She might have been worth finishing a bottle with if she wasn't so high in the instep. But that's what chaperones were. Gatekeepers here to stop all fun.

"Yes, truly sad." He gulped the ruby red liquor and relished in it. His betrothed was not his by choosing, but his father's choice, to continue the wealth of the family. Hester Montberry had been a cousin twice removed, from a side of the family that oozed wealth through its shipping of slaves to the New World. A trade that left a sour taste in his mouth. Hester had been young, attractive in a sense and not overly fond of animals, especially wild ones like the one he befriended. Her lack of love for furry creatures surprised and dismayed him. He realized then his marriage would be one for procreation of the family only, except he wasn't sure how he could sire a child with such a cold woman.

In the long run, he never had to find out. She died within a fortnight of their engagement. He realized he didn't know her enough to miss her as a person, but just as a woman who lacked warmth among other virtues.

"You lost much in that month."

"Yes, my father also perished. Surgeon claimed his heart simply stopped, after he fell off that mount. It was stated my paternal grandfather's heart also abruptly stopped one day, though my grandmere said it was his sinfulness that caught up to him." He gave her a smile. "I was but a boy and never learned what he'd done, but it must've been truly grand to die that way."

"Yes, well," the chaperone said, shifting in her seat. The story of his grandfather's infidelity often set respectable women in a tizzy. "I expect this week will be lacking such colorful tales."

"Lady Lockhart, have no fear. I have other arrangements for the men who will be here and at the gathered events, plenty of servants and loyal chaperones like yourself, to keep all mischief at bay." He raised his glass as a salute to his statement and downed the contents, hoping that would rid him of the elderly lady.

Her gaze narrowed, but she did nod. "Good. On that, my lord, I'll bid you a good night."

He watched her leave the room, barely using the cane because her temper flared at the idea he wasn't exactly stalwart on an uneventful week for her dependents. He slumped into the chair and pinched the bridge of his nose., He was beginning to question his acquiescence to his sister for this house party when the side door swung wide open, as if a tempest raged on the other side. And it did, as Ewan and two other men bounced into the room.

"Rockford, we're here!" They were red-cheeked, their clothing slightly mussed, as if running and racing about the countryside and imbibing at every tavern.

It was going to be one hellish week.

Anne led them to the rooms near the end of the hall. She opened the door and invited them into one of the pinkest rooms Marina had ever seen. The walls were pink, the drapery pink, the Aubusson carpets were mauve with pink and the bed linens were the same shade. While Marina liked the color, this was entirely too much.

"Oh, my," Ruth mumbled. Anne laughed.

"I know, I know. I was going through a pink phase then, mama said." She grinned broadly and then it vanished. "If it's too much—"

"No, it's fine." Marina didn't want to appear to be a difficult guest. When Ruth opened her mouth, Marina was sure it was to protest. She nudged her cousin. "We'll be fine here. Thank you."

"If pink was the rage then," Ruth started. She looked around. "What color was next?"

Anne laughed. "I wasn't given the chance to find out. They sent me to my cousin's house near Town."

Before the death of her parents upset their hostess, Marina noted. A truly sad note she'd not dwell on.

She didn't have to worry about upsetting Anne. She fluffed a pillow and headed toward the door, saying, "Tomorrow all the festivities will start. The modiste will arrive for fittings for the week, then we shall all go to the dance master…"

Oh, my, Marina gasped. She didn't know she was to purchase clothing here. In her mind, she re-counted her coins and prayed she could simply avoid the whole morning. She noticed Ruth's equally troubled face. As did Anne.

"Ladies, have no worry. This isn't for new apparel, unless you'd like that. It is simply a chance to trim up or add to what you have. Nothing to fret about."

"Are we the last to arrive?" Ruth asked quietly.

Their hostess gave them an impish smile. "For the ladies, yes. Again, nothing to fear."

"Our horse went lame…" Marina started, a dire need to apologize for their lateness driving her, but her cousin cut her off when she took a step closer to Anne with a wicked smile of her own.

"Did *he* come?"

Anne's cheeks reddened. She gave a sharp nod and both girls started laughing. Marina was lost, slightly miffed she had no idea of whom they spoke.

"Yes," Anne said. "But Phineas claims he'll have him too busy to see me." She delivered a perfect pout. Though Marina decided Anne had developed it to get what she wanted, because she could not see where the girl lacked anything. The pink room was evidence. Right now, what Anne wanted was a particular man, one of whom the marquis did not approve.

Ruth scrunched her nose and gave a conspiratorial smile. "Well, the week isn't done yet." They both giggled before Anne swept from the room.

Marina frowned as Ruth turned to face her.

"What, my dearest Marina? Have you eyes for Viscount Featherton?"

"That's who she's set her cap for? I thought Lord Featherton was just like his name suggests. Flighty as a bird." She plopped herself onto the settee, exhausted and slightly amused. Ewan Featherton was handsome but mentions of him in the gossip rags eluded to a not so promising match. Of course, their host was named in the rags as well. However, unlike Featherton, the debonair and dark Marquis of Rockford frequented the gaming hells and rarely the soirees. The marquis was the talked about match of the upcoming season. She sighed resignedly.

"I heard that." Ruth rushed to the chair and sat

next to her. "She has set her sights on Featherton, but I think you need to set yours on the Marquis of Rockford and what a prefect place for us to be but at his country estate." She leaned closer. "At a house party where anything could happen." And she winked.

Marina couldn't help but laugh. "I know you are doing your best to lighten my dismal future and for that, I thank you. But the marquis will be entertaining all of us here and from what I've read, he and Featherton and their group are well above our station."

"Oh, poppycock," Ruth snapped back, starting to take the hairpins out of Marina's hair. "At Christmastide, anything can and will happen. You watch."

"No mischief Ruth, please. Poor Aunt Clare could never stand for that."

"Of course not," she stated, yanking the next hairpin rather forcibly. "Oh, I'm sorry, Marina. I'd never do anything that is anything but respectable." Then she giggled.

As her long dark black hair tumbled down, Marina glared at her cousin and saw how the girl was simply having too much fun, gigging her on. She laughed with her and after a minute of finally breaking down, they both found themselves on the settee, in tears from the merriment.

After a moment, they panted, exhausted from the ride and the laughter. Marina looked at her and gave a weak smile. "We will see, Ruth. We will see."

Chapter Three

Two days later

PHINEAS RAN HIS FINGERS THROUGH his hair, tired, exasperated and nigh ready to explode. This was the holiday season, one to think of the birth of the Christ child and a festival meal to celebrate. Perhaps a party, maybe two. A house party, though, in retrospect, was beyond the pale. He had no patience for it.

He settled back in his chair at his desk in the library and sighed. This was all his fault. That little minx of a sister had again, managed to squeeze past his rules of nothing big and turned a holiday get together, soiree even, into a huge mess of too many guests and too many activities. The worst for him was finding ways to keep her and Ewan apart.

"Lord Rockford, may I have a moment?"

He glanced up and found Edward Lancashire, Earl of Riverbend, at the doorway. The tall, thin Earl, with his crooked nose from too many fights, his strawberry blond hair that never remained confined to the current style for men despite all the pomade and his brown dancing eyes could always make Phineas laugh.

"Stop sounding like a buffoon and enter, please." He waved to the chair and he stood to pour them both a brandy.

"Buffoon you say? And who is the one pouring brandies at this hour?" The gangly lord sat.

"Well, when one is dealing with Anne and her passions…"

"You mean Ewan? Or the archery?" Riverbend took the glass and nodded thanks.

Phineas's brows rose. "New fight?"

Riverbend frowned.

"The nose, boy. Looks freshly broke." He took a sip of the brandy. It was good French stock. He'd bought it from a pirate who docked up nearby. If he was going to be confined during the holidays, he'd drink the best.

"Ummm, French," Riverbend noted after his sip. He gave Phineas a sly grin. "Set up the very best stores, I see." He set the glass down. "Nose is fine. Last confrontation was two weeks ago. Bloke never stood a chance."

"No fights this week, if you don't mind." Phineas knew Riverbend's temper could go short quickly, hence the fights. His warning held a double edge and Edward knew it, for any fisticuffs would get him ousted from one of the largest parties in Rockford. Well, the only one, hence the warning.

"Of course, would never dream of it."

Phineas narrowed his gaze. Last thing he needed, but on the other hand, he could use the help. "Good. And as to the object of my concern, I'm more concerned about her infatuation with Ewan."

"Does the sot return it?"

Phineas grimaced. "Yes, I'm afraid so."

Riverbend grinned broadly and leaned forward, putting his empty glass on the desktop. "Smashing!"

That made Phineas glare.

"I fail to see what the issue is. Isn't the viscount a friend of yours? If so, wouldn't it be grand to have a brother-in-law you can tolerate, even welcome with open arms?"

"When was the last time you were with Ewan? He's nigh on twenty-five…"

"Oh, and you're his senior, by say, a few months? You call yourself a man, the great Marquis of Rockford!"

That irritated him further. "You don't understand. Yes, he's my age, but he has no responsibilities of his own, no estate worthy of her, no…"

Riverbend gave him a questioning look. "He is a man, with status, wealth that is assured through profitable estates, both here and in the West Indies, and correct me if I'm wrong, but isn't Stonebrook his?"

The property was next to his, Phineas gritted his teeth. "Yes."

"Then, son, what ails you?"

"I," he started and stopped. He shoved his chair back and started to pace. "She's not even had her debut. I know what he's like, the way he drinks, the way he throws money at the gaming hells and the whores he frequents. He is beneath her!"

"But he's your friend?" Riverbend snorted. "All right, all right. I'll help you detain his pursuit as much as I can. Let her have her Season, but Rockford, if she wants him and he her, the match is suitable as far as I can see. And I'm sure I won't be alone."

Phineas glared. "You're not helping me." He

pinched his nose bridge again. It was a bad habit but so was this debate. "All right. I won't pull them apart as to not seeing each other, but I will not allow any advances I can't have stopped. She's too young."

"Agreed. Now, when is the hunt?"

That evening...

MARINA SLIPPED DOWN THE HALLWAY, her heart racing madly. The ladies were on a scavenger hunt. Anne had handed them a list of items to search for in the house. Things like the maid's pantry, the looking glass that faced west, the locked tea caddy and other various items, nothing easily found in a house this large. The goal was to find everything before the men returned from their outing and in their search, not to disturb anything. That included the cook making dinner and Mr. Hinds, the butler, from his tasks because Anne was sure her brother would be upset. Ruth had laughed. Marina, tired from being poked and prodded again by the modiste, didn't care, but for her cousin's sake, she forced a smile and took her list to find.

By now, they were running out of time, according to the bell that Anne said would mark the end. So far, Marina had found all except for one thing, and that was the last book in the library. It didn't take her long to find the library door. But it was shut, and she pondered if she should even try it. Surely, it was open. After all, didn't everyone have the same list? With that notion, she put her hand on the door handle and twisted the release.

The door swung open to a room mostly in the dark. It was grand, from what she could tell. Big windows across from where she stood exposed the clear and starry night, not a dash of snow in sight. She stood still for a moment, to let her eyes adjust to the darkness, a room whose only light came from the low-lying embers glowing in the fireplace and the light of the stars through the windows. As the interior became clearer to her, she saw the heavy wood paneling, the dark drapes hanging to the side of the windows and the large desk that matched the walls in color. The bookshelves lined the walls except for the side the desk was poised at, near the windows and close to the fireplace.

Marina gave a heavy sigh of disappointment. Finding the last book was mind boggling. Her paper with the list of items and the pencil to mark them off, fell to the floor. She'd lost, and she knew it. Her shoulders slouched.

"Now, nothing could be that dismal," a deep, sensual male voice stated.

Stunned, her eyes shot open and she spun in the direction from which it came. In her haste, she hit a bookstand, knocking five tomes to the floor with a loud smack.

"I, I beg your pardon?" she sputtered, startled. She hadn't seen a soul when she entered. Particularly, not the one standing up from the stuffed chair near the fireplace, a glass with some liquid in it still in his grasp. "I'm very sorry. I didn't mean to intrude. We're having a scavenger hunt," she squirmed, feeling pinned to the spot. With a tight smile, she added, "This room is the library, is it not?"

The man's brows rose before he snorted. "Yes, I do believe you've found it."

She swallowed hard. The sensual voice, that sounded so smooth that it caressed her ears like a kiss, was attached to a man equally as enticing as the sound of his tongue. Tall with broad shoulders, narrow waist and elegance exuding from him. His brown hair looked bronze against the firelight and those eyes—they were blue, like light sapphires that sparkled in the same light. Square jawline, he simply was the most handsome man she'd ever seen. He made her promised beau, Lord Goodwood, even more porcine.

Eyeing his handsome form left her speechless and the acknowledgement of that played across his face.

"Cat got your tongue, my dear?"

Her mouth was too dry to even form words.

"Let's start with something easy," he said. "What are you to find?"

"Oh," that jogged her mind back into sensibility. "The last book here."

"The last book? Is that how its stated, or is it the "Lost" book?"

"Again, my lord, you have me." She felt all flustered and out of place. She'd no one to blame but herself for that. Once her father had told her the 'good news,' of her marriage proposal she'd sulked for three days and vowed to never go out again. Until this invitation arrived…

He picked up the book on his chair. "The Lost Colony," he announced. "Written by," he glared at the dark red leather cover and muttered, "Some bloke from hither." He handed it to her. "Good for a scavenger hunt, but not worth the paper it is written on." He handed it to her.

She stared down at the book's cover to avoid looking into his eyes. They were faceted like sapphires but warm and inviting. Mesmerizing, actually. It unsettled her nerves. Refocusing on the cover, she saw it was made of brown leather with the title in gold. What caught her eye was the author's name. Simply stated, it was Phineas Huntington. No title, nothing more than a name. She blinked.

"You wrote this?" Puzzled, she looked at him.

He raised a brow. "You believe I'm Phineas? What if I'm Walter Smith?"

"Who are you?" Her confusion mired her thinking. Only Phineas she had heard of recently was the marquis here. This couldn't be him. She'd heard he wasn't amiable. More of a recluse since his betrothed passed so suddenly. He only visited the gaming hells, the brothels and other such vices. He'd never be at his estate, entertaining one of the ladies of his sister's party.

"Perhaps I'm Walter Smith," he said, his voice low, almost a whisper laced with a thread that seeped down her spine and lit little hellfires along the way. Even now, it was like he caressed her, a strange feeling since no man had ever touched her other than in a brotherly way. Worse yet, he hadn't moved closer. The room was getting stuffy and she found breathing was hard.

"I don't believe you," she forced out and prayed that sounded even. Her vision was blurred she was totally convinced and her blood pounded in her ears.

He leaned back with a casual grace, like a feline all proud and assured. "I see. You are correct. I'm not Walter Smith, and yet, I am."

His masculine voice, deep and alluring, coiled down her spine. At the moment, the only thing she wanted him to do was kiss her, which was entirely outlandish, but the hunger was there. Well, at least on her part…

"I don't understand," she sputtered, trying desperately to get hold of herself.

He gave her a deeply resonate chuckle. "I write as a Walter Smith of sorts. No one would pick up a marquis's book, unless it held the meanings of life, how to cure the plague, or contained material too intimate for young eyes like yours." He smiled.

Somehow, she managed to swallow. "I see." She sounded like an idiot. "Well, let me note I found it…"

He plucked the list from the floor and tilted it in the firelight. "Ah, by no means will that do." He pulled a pen off the desk and scribbled on the page. "There, that should answer it."

She glanced at the list. His signature was bold and frank across it. *Phineas Huntington, Marquis of Rockford*. It wasn't right or proper but scrawled like a lover signing a document to be presented in court or such. It wasn't helping her gain control of her senses one bit.

"I need to go," she whispered, though her feet felt weighted to the floor.

"Yes, you do."

The words were soft, subtle and alluring. Her blood was on fire and she had no way to understand what was happening but the marquis, standing but a hairs-width away from her, leaned over and kissed her.

Chapter Four

MARINA COULDN'T BREATHE. DIDN'T WANT to breathe. The moment he leaned closer, she inhaled deeply in surprise. And when his lips touched hers, her heart skipped a beat. A voice inside her head told her to run. The core of her being refused to move. When he pressed further, and the tip of his tongue traced her lips, she believed she'd swoon. He didn't push for more when she didn't yield, but then, was she supposed to? Her thoughts were a jumble, her heart which started again, now took off at a fast pace, her ears plugged from its thudding. Slowly, her lips yielded to him and his tongue invaded her mouth for a deep kiss and then he backed away. She stood, breathless, trembling and her eyes widened in surprise.

Only one other time had she been kissed. It was a rather nice surprise with dull results. The rector's son, at one of the summer picnics, had pecked at her lips as part of forfeits for a croquet match. They were twelve and it was exciting and awkward. The group had had to race through their game and the forfeits, more so on the forfeits, before their parents found them simply because they were too young. The boy, Jeremiah, had almost missed her lips and left an interesting, somewhat bad impression on her. Afterward, she and the other girls decided kissing was not for them. Anything beyond just lips made them squeal in disgust.

This, though, was entirely different. This time, her heart raced, she grew hot and her nerves twitched in the most unusual ways. She didn't know what to think, except perhaps not to think and simply let her body do the talking. However, what it wanted made her lightheaded.

As quickly as he took her lips, he released them. The motion made her rock on her feet and that heady feeling made her stagger just a half step. He tilted his head. She noticed his blue eyes looked dark, almost navy in color, and she couldn't understand how that could happen. Kissing did that? He gave her a lopsided grin and that was all she could take. Grabbing her list, she gathered her skirts and ran.

What the hell did he just do?

He kissed her. His sister's friend. An eligible lady, one who'd be shopping for a husband, regardless of what she sputtered now. And what did he do? Attempted to compromise her here, in his own house, and put an end to all the speculation and emptiness…

He stood, inhaling a fragrance that lingered. One she wore. Lilacs. As lovely as the lady…

Instantly, he snapped out of those thoughts and went to pour himself another drink. For all that was holy, he'd come close to making a colossal mess. Worried about his sister and Ewan, was he?

He shook his head before he downed the whole glass.

No, he had to avoid her. Avoid all of them! He settled back down and began to devise his strategies for this party and keeping Anne from any time alone with Ewan. In addition, he had to plan how to avoid all the ladies before he found himself engaged…

The Next Morning…

"WAKE UP, COUSIN! WAKE UP!"

Marina tried to ignore the command but when the mattress buckled under Ruth's landing on it, she gave up and squinted her eyes, refusing to open them fully. The sunlight, streaming through the window, was hurtful to sleepy eyes.

"What time is it?"

"It's close to ten, which means we need to be up and about," Ruth chattered, bubbling with an enthusiasm that Marina could barely find inside herself.

With a deep sigh, she threw the covers back and couldn't stifle the yawn that came. Instantly, she worried her lips were swollen, because last night, she'd sworn they were bruised from the way they felt, but Ruth said nothing then or now. Perhaps she just imagined the whole thing. It wasn't real. But as she climbed out of bed, she saw the book *The Lost Colony* sitting on the chair near the fireplace and she inwardly groaned.

How was she going to behave when she saw

him? The truth was, he had taken liberties with her he shouldn't have, yet would she have denied him? He was too handsome, too alluring to simply ignore. And the kiss, the kiss was like a dream. The memory of it lingered and it was a sense she didn't want to lose though as she wiggled her toes before standing, she knew she had to. It wasn't fitting, particularly since she was doomed, no waiting, for another.

Stretching her arms and her back, she asked, "What fun are we to have today?"

Ruth giggled. "You know." She leaned closer. "Its dancing lessons. For the ball this week!"

Marina stood at the washbasin and splashed water on her face. Dance lessons. A tingle curled down her spine, a tingle of excitement and fear. Dancing meant men, and at the marquis's house, that included the man himself. Another handful of water crashed into her face. Wiping her eyes with the back of her hand, she muttered, "Oh, yes." She sputtered water back into the bowl. "I had forgotten."

Once she was dressed, Ruth grabbed her hand and down they went. Marina laughed with her cousin, though in the back of her mind, she tried to ignore the vision of a handsome marquis and how she'd love to dance with him.

Ewan's horse inched up on Phineas' beast as the two barreled around the tree in a mad dash towards the stable. Inside his head, Phineas knew he should let his friend win the contest. Especially since the marquis was doing everything within his power to keep the young lord away from Lady Anne. But the stallion beneath him was way too competitive and despite the tight reins, Midnight broke into another gait and retook the lead without too much tension from Phineas. The marquis, too, wasn't accustomed to losing, even though better judgment argued otherwise.

The two horses skidded to a stop near the stable doors and within seconds, the stable boys raced out to grab the horses' reins.

"Wasn't particularly giving, now, were you, ole man," Ewan guffawed, sliding off his horse.

Phineas leapt off his horse, giving a rub to the stallion's withers with a "good boy" whispered to the equine. To his friend, he laughed. "Thought about throwing in the cravat, but Midnight would have none of it."

"That horse will throw you one day, and it'll take the angels from heaven to put you back together again." Ewan dusted his breeches to rid the dust from them as the other gentlemen rode up.

"You two left us at the pond," Lord Smitherton griped.

"Yes, good work, my lord! Stunning victory," Lord Lorrance chimed in.

"You know, I play to win, gentlemen." Phineas forced a smile as he tucked the riding crop under his arm.

"The question being," Ewan began. "Which lady do you have in mind? We would all hate to get in your way and rejection is only acceptable when the rules are known ahead."

"I'm not searching," Phineas growled.

Ewan laughed as they walked to the mansion. "On that, we will see."

The other men chuckled, making Phineas scowl. Though in the back of mind, he was still plagued by the lady he met last night. The mere suggestion in his memory of her beauty and those ruby lips, which tasted so sweet, made his insides tighten. Nearing the house where the ladies were didn't improve his disposition.

As he and the men shuffled into the house, his heart thudded faster and breathing suddenly became harder. What he needed was a break from all this commotion. They were to clean up and head out to the village for a lords' afternoon out, to let the ladies continue preparing for the ball he prayed he could avoid. Reality was, he wanted to get back on Midnight and race into woods, to his retreat and check on his mischievous little fox. His worry for her increased with the hunt on the next day…

Music drifted out the front door the closer they got, followed by a wave of women laughing. Phineas noticed the men picked up their step, making him want to growl again. Ladies of the *ton*, at his house, to celebrate the holidays with him and the lords with him. Inwardly, he groaned, because he'd have to keep an eye out on them all before any mischief began…

He came to an abrupt halt when the chatter quieted, and they stood at the doorway to the ballroom. Inside, the ladies swirled as the dance mistress who faced the students, presenting her backside to the portal, called instructions. Phineas snorted, straightening himself upright at recognizing her.

This dance mistress, Lady Forrest, had taught him to dance when he was younger. As they'd practiced the dance steps, he'd worked on seducing her. Memories of that wild afternoon made him smile.

"My lord, what a pleasure to have you and your guests arrive!"

He blinked and snapped his attention back to now, only to find every eye was on him, including his gentlemen friends. Amazing how this instructor could feel his presence, enough to pull him into the attention he wanted to avoid. Well, perhaps she wasn't magical by feeling him there, leaning against the doorframe, but noticed the men and caught a reflection of him in the paneled looking glass pieces that decorated the side walls.

He nodded his head, his arms akimbo. "Lady Forrest, I see you've been teaching the finer things. Wonderful, as always."

She returned the smile. All he could see was her dark ebony hair so tightly pulled back that very few tendrils escaped. And her ruby red lips, décolletage and the curved hips that even the silk empire dress couldn't hide, hinted at the personal treasures she had to share. But, she was also a good stone more than most of his encounters and her years over him made her the oldest he had parlayed with.

"Well, my lord, your timing is simply superb!" She walked up to the group.

Out of the corner of his eye, he could see that Ewan and the rest were staring at the young ladies like wolves in heat that ran across females primed for them. The worst, he decided, was that the ladies were not giving them any sort of cold return. A couple looked like they were giggling in their small sets, a few were like his sister and blushing. He inwardly shook his head. The eight-year age gap between him and Anne seemed more like twenty at this moment. Twenty-one and beautiful, Anne would have suitors fighting for her hand, he decided, and there, the selection could be made with a sensibility to her welfare, the family and all that stock that marriages were to be. Ewan should have competition…

Then his gaze found her. The nymph from last night. She stood to the side with another girl and they appeared to be in deep contemplation of what was going on. The yellow gown she wore glowed as if she were an angel and on that, he'd have to agree. Her ebony locks curled around her face, adding to her virginal charm. But those grey eyes once they locked with his, set his inner control amok. While he maintained a lazy lord stance, his insides ignited. Good grief, he had to get out of here!

"Lord Rockford, if you please."

He frowned and turned toward the dance mistress. "How may I be of service, my lady?"

She smiled and coaxed him with her hand. Reluctant to want to give in, it'd be ungentlemanly to deny her aid. Once he reached her, she posed him in front of her and queued up the string artist on the side.

"My lord," she murmured and set her frame in position to dance. He frowned. Dance?

Marina had managed to push the memory of last night's heated kiss to the back of her mind with all of Ruth's babbling and the quick scone and tea she'd downed for breakfast. Her preference for fruits and eggs or anything more had to be pushed aside when their dance mistress, Lady Forrest, arrived. At first, Marina was in no mood to go through the motions, but Lady Forrest had convinced them that a good practice would shake the dust off their steps and make the evenings even more entertaining.

Her re-introduction to dancing at first was a little awkward. She knew the dances but found, like the rest, that several months away from any formal dance made her movements stilted, awkward and even she had to admit she'd forgotten a few. But the dance mistress gave them room to recall and laugh about it all. As the morning rolled on, so did the ladies. They acted in both positions, quietly joking amongst themselves that while this wasn't unusual at country dances or assemblies, this house party had enough gentlemen they should have no problem. As they laughed about that, the dance mistress's voice rose to get their attention and as she got louder, the tone turned more direct.

"Well, my lord, your timing is simply superb!"

The ladies silenced and turned. Marina gulped when she saw him. The man she'd worked so diligently to forget now stood brazenly at the doorway to the room. Instantly, the heat seemed to climb because she suddenly felt very hot. She wanted to tug at her collar, only to realize the empire gown had none around her neck. Inwardly, she moaned. It took every ounce of energy to school her body to not resemble the total collapse inside her skin.

She couldn't hear the words exchanged between

the two but when he walked out onto the dance floor with their dance mistress, Marina's eyes were glued. They went through the motions of a dance. It was one of the dances they'd practiced today, minus the partners, as if paired down to the two of them. Marina studied and watched him move with grace, feline like, how she'd imagine a lion would move. She found herself envious and that shook her. As they swayed on the floor from one step to another, she got lost in watching him. By the end, everyone applauded, even the gentlemen.

"Did you see the marquis sway? Oh, my," her cousin swooned, fanning herself with her hand.

Marina still couldn't pull her gaze away from him. With a snort, trying to play down her obvious stare, she replied, "He is, no doubt, quite practiced in the dance. He is older and has been to countless balls."

"You are right, I'm sure," Ruth panted, still trying to fan herself.

At that moment, the marquis, who had left the dance mistress and was talking to his sister, Anne, scanned the room and when his gaze found Marina, he stopped. Marina's heart jumped when his stunning blue eyes locked onto hers. The man who had so abruptly kissed her now was obviously staring at her. Marina's cheeks warmed, and she feared she'd need a fan as well. The attention unnerved her, but why wasn't so easy to gather. The heat of his gaze made her toes curl, wondering what else he might do if he kissed her again. Then, she noticed not only did the Marquis of Rockford stare at her, but so did his sister. Anne frowned.

Suddenly embarrassed, she prayed the floor

would open and swallow her whole.

⸙

Phineas did not want to dance, but how could he deny Lady Forrest? Once the music began and the twinkle in her eye caught his attention, he chuckled. This dance mistress was always the belle of the dance floor and he knew her knowledge of the dance would make this a more enjoyable demonstration than not. As the tune picked up in beat and he swayed her around the floor, he realized he did enjoy dancing.

At the end, through the applause, he bowed to the mistress then turned to take the men to leave when Anne grabbed his arm, pulling him to the side.

"What is this I'm told? That the ball will not be tonight, if at all?"

He frowned. He'd meant to tell her later, but he'd lay coin Ewan was the culprit. "Anne, please…"

"No, you've managed to keep us apart. We have behaved with all respect and politeness of unknown strangers. But this is too far," Anne seethed. She always amazed him, how she could carry an argument but from the view across the room, she'd appear to be easily conversing. Thank heavens, women were not political!

"I thoroughly agree. You two have been on your best behavior. But this is an event without as many patrons to watch over your ladies, to protect them, other than myself…"

"Fiddlesticks!" She muttered. "All the ladies have their chaperones. You, though, are the one you're more worried about." She nodded her head to the side. "Found your new match yet? For Lady Marina has been intently watching you. I'd dare say, even swooning."

He'd found his nymph, but once Forrest coerced him to stay, he'd concentrated on the dance and tried to forget the beauty whose lips were as soft as any he'd ever felt, and she'd tasted as sweet as the petit-fours they'd served at supper. The lady had invaded his peaceful slumber with their kiss hinting at the passion he'd like to take her to… and it had been that very thought, combined with Anne and Ewan, that made him put an end to any social soiree where he might find himself wrapped in her aura again.

Of course, he should've realized Anne would be less than pleased. Irate was the monster before him. He grimaced.

"We merely need to postpone it, till after the hunt." He gave an attempt at a smile, to hopefully break her scowling demeanor. "And, perhaps, the ladies would like to join us."

"On a hunt? When did you change your view that women should be left at home, eating petite-fours and gossiping?"

She'd assessed his view correctly. How was he to save this? "Anne, you enjoy riding, as I'm sure many of your guests do and—"

Her eyes widened. "And with us present, the men might be distracted enough to miss your pet?"

He was speechless. In reality he hadn't thought that far, but it would help. Before he could say a word, his sister jumped back in.

"Very well. I'll agree to the schedule change."

She leaned forward and whispered in his ear. "And perhaps, you'll tell me why Lady Marina has her sights set on you."

He turned in the direction she motioned with a nod and found the nymph. Just seeing the beauty tightened his insides. Yes, the solution to avoiding her dissolved to ash in placating his sister. Now, if he could just bury the burn this lady started deep inside him, he might escape but his heart screamed for him to stop.

Dear Lord, Saint Michael and Saint George…

Chapter Five

IT TOOK ALL EVENING FOR Marina to catch her breath. Dinner was a loss to her, as the marquis sat but ten seats from her at the table, looking very dapper in his evening attire, talking to the guests near him. When he laughed, his eyes appeared to dance in the candlelight and his grin was infectious. She did her best not to watch him and constantly reminded herself that he wasn't looking for a wife and that she, in theory according to her father, was to be tied to another. Of course, if she attracted another suitor, like the marquis, then that shipper would be out, she was sure. But, how could she attract a man of such high rank as the marquis? Without a doubt, half the ton would be seeking his attention when the Season started…

Somewhat withdrawn at that thought, she determined to forget him and chatted with the ladies near her. The one lord close to her, Viscount Featherton, did join in their discussion, but she found his gaze often went down the table, focusing on Anne, or perhaps Lady Edith Carrington, who sat next to Anne. The viscount was never rude, but it was certain he would never vie for Marina's hand, so she tried to avoid rudely gawking at the marquis and tried to pretend to eat dinner. It was an utter disaster.

After supper, the men excused themselves for brandy and the ladies went to the parlor for sherry. When Lord Rockford left the room, the pressure on her lifted and now, she was hungry—just as they took the food away. Quickly, she filched a hunk of bread and stuffed it in her shawl and hoped no one questioned why she wasn't wearing it.

"Ladies, if I may please," Anne started as they took their seats. "Our ball has been postponed until Saturday."

Groans rose from the crowd and she raised her hand to quiet them. "Yes, I know, but all is not lost. My brother has invited us to ride along with them during their hunt tomorrow." She smiled broadly.

Ruth nearly jumped from her seat. "Oh, dear! How exciting!" She turned to Marina. "We'll have so much fun!"

Marina frowned. "When did you become such a horsewoman? As I seem to recall, you mentioned carriages are the way we should travel and to leave the poor to the horses."

Ruth laughed and lightly mimicked a punch at her cousin's arm. "I was joking. We are in the country, of course we must ride!" She paused. "You are the one who enjoys the canter. This must make you pleased."

"You are correct. But to ride while they look for a fox, which is cousin to the dog, doesn't seem right. Hmmmm," she pondered. "Of course, I could try to dissuade them from firing at the animal."

Ruth laughed hard. "By all means though I have my doubts that will work."

Anne stood at the front, a glow on her face caught Marina's attention. "She looks overly pleased."

"It is a chance for her to be with her viscount." She lowered her tone and added, "The marquis does not want her to be courted by him. They are, unofficially, of course, courting. 'Tis quite the scandal."

The handsome marquis did not want his sister with a viscount? That would explain the separated entertainment and possibly explain why the ball was pushed to the end of the party. It made her wonder, if the man was that determined, why let them come on the hunt? He was a mystery and one who, unfortunately, intrigued her.

The Next Morning…

PHINEAS MOUNTED HIS HORSE, HIS mind filled with a flurry of thoughts that had him on the verge of a headache, which was the last thing he needed right now. As the stallion sidestepped when Phineas turned him, the crowd behind them was growing. The men were already there, having had breakfast, and on top of their mounts. A couple of them were checking their guns. The excitement in the air sizzling. Hunts always invigorated him, and it did his male guests as well. They did grumble when he informed them the ladies would accompany them. After a moan or two from the dozen men there, Ewan had piped in how grand it would be for the ladies to witness them in action, as a showpiece of their skills, an appreciation, he added, that might fetch a dance or two with a favored lady. That prospect made the men cheer and Ewan grinned. The young buck had behaved but this was exactly why Phineas had postposed the ball. Until he could find a way to get Lady Margaret Kimball, Anne's appointed chaperon, to keep a closer eye on her charge, he'd have to figure another way…

"Here, here! Welcome, ladies!" Ewan barked. A round of applause by all the men filled the stable yard. Phineas glanced up and found Anne leading the ladies to the mounting blocks.

Anne sat on her sidesaddle so primly, Phineas couldn't help but smile. He'd taught her how to ride, granted they were children and they rode bareback and astride—before Mr. Bender, his father's manservant, discovered them and his father put an abrupt end to that practice. After that, she was taught to ride sidesaddle, the 'accepted' manner for ladies. With her back straight and her seat right, she looked fine and he grinned… until he noticed Ewan grinning also. His scowl returned.

"My lord, the hounds?"

He blinked and looked down at the servant. *Heavens, no!* Not all the hounds. But not taking any, to protect his little furry friend Petunia, would not make sense. He had trained one of the dogs not to sniff for Petunia, which had taken him over a week to achieve. One hunting dog, though, might make him appear weak and he couldn't have that. With a deep sigh, he replied, "Bring Mattie and Brutus."

A look of surprise flashed across the servant's eyes before he mumbled 'my lord' and left to fetch the hounds. Two would have to work. Brutus would follow Mattie anywhere and he'd made sure the bitch wouldn't hunt Petunia, or so he hoped.

"Only two?" Ewan commented when he rode

up. "A bit off, wouldn't you say?"

"They are my best," he quickly replied. "Besides, Max and Smiley are off their game, since Saxon went into heat."

"Only lord I know who uses males and bitches to hunt with."

Phineas laughed. "And my kills from such hunts, are they lacking?"

Ewan shook his head. "How they aren't, I'm not sure. With two females in the pack, you'll have fireworks!"

Phineas opened his mouth to make another remark when he saw her. Miss Lockhart was the fourth rider back, and was so beautiful on horseback, his mouth went dry. She wore a navy riding habit with her long and luscious dark hair pulled back in a knot that was desperately trying to unravel. Like the other ladies, she held a riding crop in one hand and it dangled loose, as if she was trying to find some discreet way to lose the piece. The way she directed her horse made his insides tighten and other parts aware of the attraction. He'd have to gather his control, or his own seat would become terribly painful indeed.

As the gentlemen quickly welcomed the ladies, he found her nodding in respect, then as she looked over the crowd her gaze found him. She tilted her head just slightly, and then her plump lips curled up on one edge. His jaw tightened. Pulling on the reins, he returned the nod and quickly turned Midnight toward the front of the group.

"Good morning, ladies and gents," he greeted. It was late morning, later than he wanted, but better for his fox, who he often found out and about in search of her food. By now, she was resting, and he prayed, this time, nowhere near here. "Welcome to the grounds of good fortune. Usual rules apply. Gentlemen, do take guard, the ladies are with us."

A cheerful murmur went through the crowd. He found himself staring at that girl again. Lady Marina Lockhart, he recalled. He had a strong urge to ride with her but restrained himself. A breeze whipped through the air as the clouds above increased. The women, dressed in their long wool cloaks, all seemed to adjust their seats, trying to snuggle into the wrap, a garment that had a hood that covered their bonnets, whereas the men sat bareheaded. Excitement flared through them enough to make them ignore the increasing cold.

Of course, Phineas worried that the weather would turn. The partly sunny, warm splash could quickly turn to winter in a heartbeat here in the country. It was December. He felt the breeze was a bit cooler than earlier, prompting him to suggest they dress accordingly. A drop of rain hit his nose, but it was minor. If the weather would hold off until they were finished, he'd be pleased. The droplet, he noticed, was slight yet the dogs were barking, and the horses' hooves clicked on the drive in anticipation. The sooner they started, the quicker they'd be back. He finally had his head horseman clang the starting bell.

The dogs took off in a madcap run into the woods, clambering over fallen trees, rocks and over undergrowth. The horses followed. The pursuit called to Phineas' inner core. He inhaled deeply, realizing how much he enjoyed this, being outside and reveling with nature. To his upper right, he saw his sister and Ewan, not next to each other but close. In the midst of the hunting party was Lady Lockhart and the one he heard was her cousin, along with two other gentlemen. After he'd counted all his chicks, or so he called the guests, it appeared all would be good. With a quiet sigh, he settled in his saddle for a pleasant hunt.

As they raced across the grounds, he noticed the minor rain drops on his coat, but the hunt was on. Then clouded skies clashed in a loud roar, skittering the horses' steps as their riders jerked. All hell exploded.

Marina had checked her appearance several times in the full-length looking glass before she and Ruth left for the hunt. She came to the conclusion she was presentable. Ruth remarked she was stunning, but she'd never go to that extreme.

There was an excitement in the air as the ladies gathered in the front hallway, to head to the stables for their mounts.

"How exciting!"

Ruth was at her side, more bubbly than Marina thought she could handle. But the cooler air and the brisk wind did wake her fully and she glanced at the group. All were in good spirits, so she smiled, deciding she'd make herself enjoy this event. She wondered where the marquis was, despite her admonishment to herself that thinking of him was useless. She was not of the class a man of his station would take to wife. Besides, she had to remind herself, unless she could attract another lord, her father would follow through with his idea to marry her to the elderly Lord Goodwood. She shivered at the thought.

Finally, she found the marquis, sitting high on his horse. He looked so handsome, he almost made her swoon...Good heavens, she thought, the man was quite vulgar, really, taking such a forward kiss and ignoring her otherwise that she needed to stop searching for him. But he had created an ache inside her that hungered for his touch. On the verge of turning her own mount around so she could see him, his gaze caught hers. Those blue eyes sparkled, even in the overcast sky. She couldn't help herself from giving him a minor smile, despite her decision she stood no chance against a high-ranking lord who sought no bride, or so he said. He noticed her and returned the same, which only made her nerves catch on fire.

"I see the marquis notices you," Ruth whispered. "You should set your cap for him."

"Don't be foolish," Marina snapped but quickly attached a snort, in hopes it sounded more like a laugh. No need to shout at the girl, who had the company of Lord Comstock at her side. "He is simply being polite."

"Lady Lockhart, don't be so sure of that," Comstock said. "We've all noticed his attention when you are present. Perhaps all is not lost."

She stared wide-eyed at the man. "Interesting. He is the host of this holiday week. I'm sure I'm not the only one he notices." And on that, she gave a nudge to her horse to move forward. Whatever would a man know about women?

Within minutes, the group was facing to the

east, the dog handlers still holding the hounds at bay, despite their pulling to be sent on the hunt. Marina looked over the horizon, toward the trees and hills, where some unexpecting fox would be chased, cornered and killed by one of these men. Despite her thrill to be able to ride, she wanted to withdraw. She wasn't sure she could witness this barbaric practice.

"Stop frowning!" Ruth hissed quietly, so only Marina could hear.

"How can I? You know I don't like this ending one bit."

"You'd rather stay and say, embroider, while all the men are here? Including that delectable one you still refuse to discuss what happened in the library with when you met him?"

What was she to say? *He kissed me, and I liked it?* Even the mere glimpse of that idea, of repeating it, sent her heart racing.

A raindrop fell on her nose. She scrunched it in surprise. Then another hit her forehead. Her frown returned. The last thing she wanted was to be perched on this mare in the rain…

Suddenly, a whistle sounded, the dogs were released, howling as they ran and that set off the herd around her. Her mare leaped into the frenzy of cantering horses as they followed the dogs. Marina's leg wrapped tightly around the sidesaddle horn, thankful her years of riding were coming back to her. In London, she had no need to ride and her father more or less forbade it, claiming ladies didn't need to sit on a beast to travel; that a carriage was the more polite and ladylike way. She stifled a groan and put her riding habits aside, so it was a thrill to be here and participate, though in a hunt, it was questionable.

More rain started to fall. It was gentle and light, but she did notice it was colder than before. The skies darkened right as the hounds rushed into the woods and they all followed. A crash of thunder clapped loudly, and the skies opened, pouring buckets downward. Marina was soaked, as was her mare and the reins. As she tried to pull back on the ribbons, to slow the mare down, the slick leather slipped through her gloved hands and she lost control, reaching for the horn through her skirts to hang on. She couldn't see in the downpour, which made matters worse. Then her mare went to hop over a fallen timber and as the horse lifted her hooves, Marina lost her grip. A scream escaped her as another clap of thunder clashed above and she fell from her mount to the ground with a thud, hitting her head on the log.

And then, her world went black.

Chapter Six

A ROAR OF THUNDER AND LIGHTNING rang through the heavens above him, and the resulting downpour made the Marquis of Rockford roar. The hounds continued on their mission and most of the group followed, but, blinking through the rain, he felt blind. He saw a few of the party bolt at first after the dogs before the blinding rain stopped them. The rest skidded to a stop by the time he got to them.

"Is everyone all right?" he shouted as another clap of thunder came. The winds picked up and the temperature grew colder by the moment. "Everyone, return to the house immediately!"

The riders turned their horses, and he could hear a mumble through the group.

"My lord!"

He squinted. It was the drenched cousin of the gorgeous lady he'd kissed. She came barreling up on her horse, looking more like a drowned rat from the rain. Rain that was slowly turning into snow. Phineas growled. Thunder snows were dangerous.

"Yes, my lady."

"My cousin, Lady Marina," the girl sputtered through the chattering of her teeth. "I can't find her."

He scanned the crowd and furrowed his brow.

"I'm sure she's close. I'll find her. Now go!"

The girl opened her mouth to protest, but one of the men grabbed her horse's reins and guided her with him on the way back to Rockford Hall. Phineas searched, but couldn't find the girl in question. Smothering the swear words that cropped up in his head, he whistled to the dogs. He'd use them to find her. The two came loping back, the elder one hopping on her legs as the snow began to thicken. It was growing uglier by the minute. He swore and ordered the dogs to find her.

In a moment, he heard them baying over the rise and urged his mount into gallop. The equine snorted, stomping in the snow to find his footing but obeyed. The dogs were pacing by the time he arrived. He slid off the stallion as the heavy snow continued to pile up on the ground. Halfway covered under the white, he found a lump of navy wool. Marina's cloak was that color. In a panic, he raced, pushing the dogs away and digging through the thick wet snow.

"Lady Marina! Marina!!" He pulled her into his arms as carefully as he could. A quick inspection found no injuries, but she was pale, cold and not responding. "Damn!" He scooped her up into his arms and looked to see where he was exactly. The falling snow was so dense, he couldn't see the hall in the distance. Maddening, as he knew it was not that far. But the coverage on the ground was piling up fast in this thunder-snow, and he strongly doubted it wise to try to take her back there on these horses. His own horse's hooves were completely covered. With a quick thought, he realized they were close to his garden house. It had a fireplace and some food if he recalled correctly. They could sit out the storm there.

Adjusting Marina in his arms, he whistled to the animals. The dogs were gone, no doubt back to the house for dinner. The horses, though, followed him. The walk was difficult, stomping through thickening snow and carrying her. His stockings were soaked, his own cape heavy as the wool absorbed the snow, his face chapped by the winds and his leather boots soggy. He'd wager she was faring no better in her ensemble, so he did his best to get to shelter quickly.

At the garden house door, he refrained from kicking the door open and managed to raise the latch without dropping her. Inside was dry but cold. He put her down, so he could start a fire. Thankfully, the gardener had put wood in the hearth and kindling close by. Phineas snorted. Apparently, his visits here were noticed. Or perhaps God had told the man to provide these necessities. If that was the case, he thanked the heavens and got the fire going.

As he turned back to his guest, he found her still unconscious and with another set of eyes on her. Petunia. The fox sat upright on the table next to the chair and stared intently at Marina.

"I wondered where you were," he greeted, taking a moment to pat the animal's head.

The fox chirped. He nodded.

"Yes, she fell off her horse. Now, let me tend to her. You can go rest."

The animal chirped again but retreated to the bedding he had for her in the corner of the room.

Phineas looked at his patient and sighed. There was a cot relatively close to the fireplace. It was comfortable enough, even he had napped on it a few times. But Lady Marina was slumped in the chair. He knew he should take her to the bed, save he'd have to get her out of those damp clothes or she could come down with an ague or worse. His skills in undressing the ladies had never been unpleasant to them, for none had complained, but this lady was different. The others he had bedded. This one… she was a beauty, enough to make his loins stir and at the mere suggestion of undressing her, his body jolted awake. He shut his eyes and refocused. Warmth or sickness, the result of what he chose stood before him wide open. With a deep sigh, he marched forward…

Her head hurt. She wasn't sure why, but above her ear, and just behind it, smarted soundly. The pain turned sharp when she attempted to move, so she didn't. She inhaled a delightful scent of fire burning and a stew cooking. Reminded her of the kitchens at home, when she'd sneak down the servants' stairs on her way to the stables. Still not opening her eyes, she enjoyed the comfort her position gave her, snuggled under the covers.

Suddenly, she felt a presence, something close by. It dissipated, and she was lulled back asleep. Something tickled her nose. Her eyelids shot open, and she found a little fuzzy red and white furred creature staring back at her. Surprised, she blinked. The little creature was still there, its little black nose twitching, a vibration that went down its white whiskers. Slowly, Marina reached out to touch the animal. She'd almost succeeded when the fox chirped, jerked back, and then scampered off. Marina squinted, trying to see where it ran, but the door to the room opened with a gust of wind whipping through the area. The cold quickly made her retreat under the blankets.

Footsteps followed, a loud stomping of two feet. The slam of the door sounded as if it was kicked shut. Marina trembled, her head throbbing as her thoughts swirled on how and where she was. She recalled in a flash riding on that mare. The rain started. Thunder and lightning ensued, causing her beast to fret. The wet reins slipped and a fast turn by her horse caused her to slide off the sidesaddle, tumbling downward then nothing. At the end, the pain in the back of her head banged loudly. Tentatively, she quietly reached to her temple and moved back to the pain and found a knot in the swollen flesh. When did that happen? The pain seemed to block her memory. She closed her eyes, attempting to force the pain to ebb.

It was then she realized she had nothing on but her undergarments. Her riding habit was draped over a chair near the fire and her boots stood next to the skirts. A flash of concern raced through her. Who had undressed her?

The kettle over the fire, which had a delicious scent, wafted past her. Whoever was here remained in the room. Feeling vulnerable and lost, she slowly peeked again and found a man bent over the fireplace. Her heart sank. A man. And a wild creature, she reminded herself. This was not good...

The man stood and slowly turned. Her eyes shot wide open. It was the marquis! She couldn't decide if she should be relieved it was him or livid because he was the only one present. She had not become unclothed by her own machinations.

"Lady Marina, good to see you're awake." He poured her a cup of water and took it to her. "Here, drink, I'm sure you're thirsty, though be careful. It's still cold." He offered her the cup.

With a narrow glance, unsure still how to take this situation, she reached out and took the cup. "Thank you." She was thirsty. One sip, though, nearly froze her again. "That is quite cold!"

He shrugged. "It has turned rather chilly out."

She gave him the cup back as she had no place to put it, grabbed the coarse, wool blanket tight and propped herself up, doing her best to remain entirely covered. But the change in her position set a stab of pain in her head. She couldn't help but wince. "What happened?"

He pressed a wet freezing cloth against the knot in her head. Another surprise. He knew it was there. She didn't complain as the cold deadened the fiery hurt.

"If you recall," he started, his fingers combing her hair away from the injury. "It started to rain, well, pour."

She frowned. She did remember that. "It thundered and lightning. Yes." She shivered. "And the wind. I remember it turned colder..." The word faded as she grabbed the blanket tight and jumped up as best she could, all bundled and went to the window, moving the closed curtain. What she saw made her heart skip a beat. It was dark out and the glass was hard to see through because it had iced. *Ice?* She whipped her head around and glared at him. "It snowed?"

He raised his brows with a shrug. "Yes, Lady Marina. Thundered and the rain turned to snow." Grabbing the poker, he stirred the fire.

"Wait, wait. Where is everyone else?"

"I assume they are back at the house. I hope that is the case. The weather turned so suddenly, and the thunder frightened the horses and many of the riders, making us all rather a mess out there." He stirred the pot, which filled the air with an enticing aroma. Her stomach growled.

"Can I interest you in stew?"

She frowned. Angry at her body for speaking, for she had to get some answers. "Wait, no—"

"No to food?" He scooped up a spoonful and put it in a bowl.

Her head started to throb again. At least, that's what she hoped was hurting. "No, not that, but how did I get here?" Stupid question, the voice in her head shouted. "On the other hand, I guess you brought me here—"

"I saw you, on the ground, partially in a puddle and halfway covered in snow, I might add, and unconscious. Of course, I collected you," he stated, rather factually, as if he was giving a lecture. She just stared. He filled another bowl. "I brought you here, because I wasn't sure if you were hurt and at that point, the snow was blinding."

"And it's here, you violated me?"

Phineas didn't look at her but filled another bowl. Last thing he needed was a lady throwing a tantrum. Even beautiful women, like Lady Marina, were prone to misunderstand. He inhaled deeply, readying himself for another accusation.

"I did not violate you."

"Oh, yes, I see. You brought me here away from anyone else and disrobed me. I consider that a violation of my person." There was fire in her eyes and that, he discovered, made his insides tighten.

"Lady Marina." He put the bowls on the small table. "This cottage was the closest shelter available. As I said, I wasn't sure if you were injured. You were unconscious. It made complete sense to bring you here for your own safety."

Her glare hardened.

He found the smaller bowl on the table and brought if to the fireplace. "Look at your gown, my lady. It was soaking wet from the rain and that puddle your horse dumped you in. It made no sense to keep you in soaking wet clothing, in the freezing cold, and think you would be well." The bowl was filled. He brought it close to Petunia, in the corner. The fox inched her way closer. Phineas grimaced. The lady's bad temper made his little one wary. He shook his head.

"Have no fear," he added. "I closed my eyes."

Her brows shot upward. "Closed your eyes? Your skills are that good, you needed no eyes to do this?"

Phineas snorted as he gave his little fox a pet. He did consider himself rather adept at disrobing a beautiful lady. But the flames coming off his guest's blazing gaze burned a hole in his back, he was sure. He rose and turned to face her.

"Lady Marina, if I had left you in your riding habit, you'd have a raging fever by now, since you'd be shivering in freezing cold and wet wool. The blankets and mattress would be ruined from the soaking garments and by far, all would be worse than you standing here, not ill but angry when you realize it was only your riding clothes and that endless petticoat you had on underneath it. You are still covered, and the sight of your arms has already been exposed to the likes of me and all, as that is the fashion." He took a step forward. "Am I not correct?"

Her gaze narrowed and those gorgeous lips of hers, the ones that he remembered were so soft and sweet tasting, gripped her mouth closed, thinning into a line. He waited. The fact that she exploded only reassured him she was going to be fine, mayhap a small knot on her head that'd fade over time.

Finally, she started to slowly nod her head. "I see. So, once my ensemble dries, what then?"

Oh, hell!

Chapter Seven

Marina was famished. She downed the first bowl and was halfway through the second when it hit her how ill-mannered she'd been. Carefully, placing the spoon down, she sat upright, still managing to keep the blanket wrapped around her. The marquis sat quietly across the table from her, petting a small red-colored dog that she could swear resembled a sheep.

"Lord Rockford," she started, trying to find the proper tone. "Please excuse my rather rash behavior. To snap at a lord, who apparently risked his life to save mine, is simply inexcusable."

His lips curved into a slight smile, but he never truly looked at her, so preoccupied with the varmint in his lap. A fox. How did he tame a fox?

"Well, the good Lord put me at the right place," he answered. Putting the animal down, he picked up his empty bowl and asked her in gestures if she wanted more.

"No, my lord. Thank you."

Phineas put his in an empty bucket. His silence was deafening. In fact, the stillness of the cottage was becoming overwhelming. She swallowed and forced herself forward in conversation.

"I think my habit is mostly dry by now. Shouldn't we consider joining your other guests?" The longer they stayed, the more damaging this situation was turning. Aunt Clare would have them betrothed before morning, if they didn't return soon, of that Marina was sure.

Lord Rockford shook his head. With even the negative look, Marina had to admire him. He moved with the grace of Olympus, she imagined. Vague shadows hinted in her head of him carrying her and the strength of his hold, the rock-hard chest and arms of iron, emblazoned in her memory. Standing relaxed here, wearing only his breeches and stockings, shirtsleeves and waistcoat, he was a vision to entice any lady. So why wasn't he married?

He broke her line of thought by opening the door. The snow was halfway up his calves and still falling from above. The chill had him quickly close the door.

"It hasn't let up. I won't risk your health, nor the safety of the horses, trying to return in all this mire…"

"I don't understand. Isn't this your gardener's cottage? As I recall, the garden, which is lovely, is just outside your back door." It was an exquisite maze as she recalled, viewing it from above, out of her bedchambers. But she also did not remember seeing a cottage of this size within it. And this one was rather large actually for a gardener's cottage.

Phineas smiled. That smile alone could make her shift from the idea of proper lady to inviting siren, she decided, rather uncomfortably.

"True. But I haven't had a true gardener in quite a few years since Mr. Hayworth passed."

"Then who manages…" His silence and the idea

made her head spin. "You act as gardener? Why?"

He shrugged. "I like watching nature, interacting with it. Digging my hands into the earth can be more enlightening than managing an estate books or the confines of the House of Lords."

"And your friend?"

"I beg your pardon?"

She pointed to the beady black eyes of the red-furred animal that sat in his arms. It was as if he'd forgotten he held the creature.

"Oh, yes," he chuckled. "Lady Marina, may I introduce Petunia."

"Petunia? You named the creature?" She took a step forward, curiosity getting the better of her.

"It seemed fitting."

"But she," she stopped and looked at him. "It is a she?" At his nod, she continued, "She is a wild animal. Surely not meant for confinement."

Before he could open his mouth, the little animal began to chatter. The noise was high-pitched and fast. It frankly scared Marina and she jerked back a space. Lord Rockford chuckled.

"I think she's trying to tell you that you are more confined than she is." He patted the furry creature.

"Aren't you afraid she'll bite you? Or, or claw at you?" Marina was simply too stunned that a lord would be his estate's gardener and have a fox for a pet.

"No."

"Wait," she ignored his reply, because none of this made sense. "We were on a fox hunt you hosted. Yet, you claim friendship of a type with the prey? Explain that to me, if you would."

He released Petunia, who jumped up on the

table and edged her way toward Marina. She held her breath, though she was fascinated. The animal was as beautiful as the paintings she'd seen in London, but this seemed odd.

"I found Petunia when she was a kit. Her mother wasn't around, probably killed in a hunt like ours today. I," he paused. "I took her in and cared for her until she was mature enough to be outside."

The fox leaned forward. Marina didn't move as the creature extended her face to sniff Marina's hand. Slowly, she moved, the urge to touch the furry animal building inside her.

"And the hunt?" Her fingers slightly grazed Petunia's fur. So soft…

"Yes, well, activities were on demand for the gentlemen and such a grand estate as this, I was pushed to allow it."

Petunia was close enough that Marina could run her hand lightly down her back. His statement, though, made her give him a questioning look. "What if the dogs had found this one? You'd allow them to shoot your pet?"

"She's not a pet. She has her freedom but, no, I wouldn't allow that." He rose and went to the corner, moving the tiny cupboard there to the side and exposing a black hole. "Her escape hatch into this cottage. I trained her to hide from us."

Surprise didn't begin to explain how she felt. "And she followed your direction? A wild animal?"

"Foxes are very smart." And on that note, Petunia leapt from the table to her little bed off to the side, licking herself furiously.

She frowned, more confused than ever about this man. He seemed to be a contradiction to himself at every turn. A marquis with substantial holdings, a bachelor who sought no bride after his fiancé died, a man who could dance with the elegance of a master but appeared to avoid all his guests if he could help it and finally, the host who had arranged a hunt but taught his fox to escape.

"Who are you?" The question formed on her lips but the falling timber in the fire snapped her back to herself and her heart sank. When he opened the door, she could see it was night. And here she was, in a cottage, apparently off the beaten path, alone with a handsome lord. This would be any other lady's dream, especially with him, with his good looks and title, but for her, all she saw was doom. Ruined by a lord who, she felt in the pit of her stomach, would never want her. She hugged the blanket tighter and sank further into the straight-back chair.

Phineas sat on pins and needles, each poking into him, when Petunia had appeared. He knew the fox was here, but he'd hoped she'd be fearful of the lady. But, then again, he had no idea the lady would be warm to his pet. He constantly had to remind himself the fox wasn't his, but she came to him in a heartbeat when he ventured into the woods. He loved the little minion, but he also feared for her.

Right now, though, his fear shifted to Lady Marina. The woman had rolled herself into that comforter as if she was a caterpillar, about to cocoon to transfer into a beauty. Yet Lady Marina needed no mold to change. She was beautiful and caring, carefully choosing her words and not screaming at the sight of Petunia, no reprimand for him for protecting her. But now, she looked as if she were in Herculaneum and Mount Vesuvius had exploded, the resigned yet frightened look etched into her skin. She was a puzzle, for no other lady he knew of would appear so calm under these circumstances.

Her question returned to his thinking and he blinked. "I'm who I've always been," he stated surely. "I just see no reason to destroy this beautiful creature just to entertain guests, guests that I did not plan to arrive."

She frowned. "But I thought this was your Yuletide House Party."

Of course she would, because that was how society ordained it to be. "No. It was at the urging of Lady Anne. I would have been content without all the silliness hosting these events brings." There, he'd said it. Though, the truth now rubbed him wrong. "Not that I am displeased to have you. It has been a pleasure, at times."

She laughed. "Yes, too many hens in the henhouse, I hear, can drive the rooster to crow."

That made him smile. "So true."

There was a pause and the air between them grew thick. He had done his best to leave her covered so as not to raise concern, but her dress was soaked to the threads and he couldn't have her get lung fever or worse because proper manners would have him keep her dressed. The blanket she wrapped herself in was an old quilt the house staff had sent to the previous gardener and Phineas found it serviceable when he was here. It wasn't in the best of condition, with stitching coming loose and a patch missing over the piece on her hip. Yet, she looked delicious and he so wanted a taste…

That jolt of desire shook him back to reality. Instantly, he got up and went to the window to take a peek out. It was still dark and cold, but the wavy glass gave no hint as to whether it was still snowing. He opened it slightly to get a better view and the icy cold hit in him the face, as did the snow. Disgusted, he slammed it shut.

"It's still snowing," he muttered over his shoulder.

Out of the corner of his eye, he saw her shudder and pull the blanket tighter. Unfortunately, that hug of quilt gave hint of the feminine body it covered, and his loins ached. He groaned.

She gulped. "What are we to do?"

He prayed. "We have to wait. It's too dark to try to return. The snow is deep. I won't risk the horses and ourselves out there in this. Surely, it'll lessen by daybreak…"

"Morning?" She gasped. "We can't stay here any longer this way!"

Ah, her calm evaporated at the thought of being with him. His jaw tightened, despite the countering argument that she had every right to do so. "Lady Marina, there's no need to worry."

"Worry? This will ruin us, I mean me! Tell me, my lord, how large a wedding shall we plan?" There was a hint of disgust in her voice, along with resignation.

He closed his eyes. "Nothing has happened between us—"

"You know that does not matter." She pulled herself up, to the perfect posture of a lady, even if dressed in a blanket. "I am ruined."

Phineas sighed. The fact she was correct didn't matter. He went to the door in the back of the room and saw her cringe, huddling deeper, when he grabbed the latch, and slipped inside. All it took was one second for him to grab the bottle and close the door again. As he walked right past her, he noticed the shocked look on her face.

"My, has it stopped snowing?" spilled form her mouth.

He popped the cork. "No, my lady, it has not." He popped the cork out of the bottle, poured into two glasses off the shelf and handed one to her.

With a puzzled look, she took a sip, never taking her eyes off him. With a snort, he went over to the trunk and opened it. He rummaged through the pieces and finally pulled out a garment.

"Here. Your dress still isn't dry. Always an issue with all those layers, I suppose." He shrugged. "May not be your correct size, but I think it's close enough to make you feel more dressed."

She downed another dainty sip before she put the glass down and took the dress. He pointed to the curtained divider that was near the wall where the Petunia's bedding sat. She shot him a worried look and he shook his head.

"Do not worry about her. Besides, she likes you enough to come greet you. Your stepping past her should be no concern."

She took gingered steps and slipped behind the curtain. Phineas poured more wine. It was going to be a difficult night. The snow was falling, locking him in seclusion with a beautiful lady. Normally, he'd be pleased, but this lady wasn't looking for a tryst. He was unnerved by her conclusion this was not going to go well. Ruination was the word, whether he touched her or not. It wasn't their fault the weather changed so dramatically but he should've know better and planned for this. Though who would've thought thunder snow after these last tempered days.

One thing was certain. He'd find a way to keep her virtue and reputation intact, but marriage wasn't the way. With his connections, surely…

Suddenly, his guest came out from behind the screen and gave him a nervous smile.

"Better, my lord?"

His mouth dropped open. Before him stood a beautiful lady, in a dress that caressed her more than it should, or what he thought. Her hair was in a tumble to the side, adding an aurora around her, like a crown. She was gorgeous. He tightened, a fire igniting within.

For the first time in a long time, Phineas finally felt trapped.

Chapter Eight

MARINA HAD THROWN THE QUILT to the side and shimmied into the dress and discovered, to her surprise, how well it fit her. The cotton sprig dress was a bit light weight for this weather, the almost sheer cotton hugging her so closely, she wondered why he kept it here. That and the wine, which was an oddity for a gardener's cottage, for it tasted too good, so refined and full of favor, not the type she'd imagine a gardener would have.

Pleased to finally be presentable again, she stepped out and found the marquis staring at her, his mouth agape. A tingle fluttered down her spine. Now what was she to do?

"Lady Marina, you are beautiful," he finally stated.

Her cheeks heated. "Thank you, but truly, my cousin, Lady Ruth, is more lovely than I." It was true. It had taken her years to realize that Ruth held more beauty than she ever could. Surely, he'd see that.

"No, on that you are mistaken."

The silence that fell was thick, like the accumulating snow outside. She wanted to snatch the quilt back up around her, but she suddenly found herself too warm, her insides melting at his gaze. Besides, her feet were glued to the floor. She found her wineglass and took a drink, letting the fruity taste burn down her throat, keeping her senses planted on that and not him.

To break the stillness, Petunia peaked out from under the hemline of her dress. Marina jumped with a shriek, which made the little fox leap to the side and closer to Lord Rockford. The marquis laughed and scooped up his little red-haired demon.

"We seem to be making a scene," he started, peering over the fox at her. "For you not to know she sneaked under there and for me not noticing she had moved."

The animal jumped out of his arms and onto the floor, licking herself furiously. Marina laughed. "She seems not to enjoy your touch, my lord."

He snorted. "'Tis not the first time a lady has run from me," he muttered before realizing he'd said it out loud. He looked at Marina in that moment and she caught a flicker there, perhaps hoping she didn't catch it. But she had.

"Is that why you're not looking for a bride here, at your own house party?"

At first, he wouldn't look at her and instead, got up to get the wine bottle. "Not at this time."

"Still," she took a sip. The wine was tasty, she absently thought, her nerves unwinding, though the fire in the pit of her belly had not cooled. "Why would you refuse to look? There are many ladies here, of good standing, all ready to make a dash this Season. Why not scoop up one now?"

"You mean, a beauty like you?"

That made her uncomfortable. "I'm not qualified." How was she to say that she was spoken for, when in reality she wasn't. It'd been a comment spoken by her father, yet many times, they were all true. He hadn't told her no Season… yet.

Lord Rockford tipped his head right. "And how, pray tell, are you not? Your family is respectfully noted in Debrett's, you are of age. Have you already accepted an offer?"

There was a pitch in his words that sounded hopeful she had not, or that's what she hoped for. "No, no offers have been made." Not to her ears. Heavens, she barely knew Lord Goodrot, no, Goodwood. What she hoped for was a man like the one before her, though she had no hopes of this highly placed lord.

He finished the second glass of wine and put it down, coming close to her. His eyes were soft and darker, like deep sapphires glowing with warmth. They were mesmerizing and held her attention. The backside of his fingers caressed her check softly.

"You are beautiful."

His voice was low, seductive and his touch lit a fire deep inside. She needed to set him back or run but the snow stopped that. The heat in her loins was new and uncomfortable. She wanted more, but wasn't sure what she wanted more of, outside his touch. He was danger and here she was, trapped with him and a fox. Her breathing was difficult, more like panting than breaths. What was she to do?

Everything that could go wrong was heading

down the dark and winding path. The wine probably was adding to it. Never had he realized that stocking this cottage with goods would come so in handy. His hideaway from the world was no longer hidden.

The lady before him was a siren, reeling him in. He hadn't wanted this party. The hunt less so. But the drastic change in weather he should've planned for. After all, who expected a warm winter would last? As the clouds had increased, he recalled the hair on his neck bristled but he'd also ignored it. At the first crack of thunder, he should've order all back to the manor. But it had turned to chaos and when he saw Marina slumped on the ground, her horse prancing nervously nearby, all good ideas fled—along with everyone else. He prayed they all made it back safely. But even the short walk here had been precarious with the snow dumping like it did and his slow gait with the injured girl.

Now, they were safe for the night, safe from the elements but really, not from the lust that stirred deep inside. What was it about this woman that enticed him so? She was beautiful. And well mannered, quiet and not as forward as his sister, Lady Anne. The dress she had donned wasn't for her but for Anne, one she'd thrown into the rag bin but one he thought still had wear in it. Why on God's green earth he had brought it here escaped him.

Perhaps it was the wine that made all measures of propriety flee. Or a longing he didn't know he had. He ran his fingers through her long dark hair, freeing it from the remaining pins so it cascaded down her back. It was a gorgeous mess of curls that reached to her hips. As his fingers circled back to her jawline and traveled to her chin, he stared into those gray eyes that were wide with wonder and curiosity. He absently wondered if those plump rosy lips had ever been kissed and he found he hoped his slight touch the other night had been her first. They were soft, he recalled that. Now, he knew they'd taste of the red wine. Oh, how he had to try. He bent forward, gently took the wine glass out of her hand and kissed her.

He was right. She did taste like the wine but with a fruitful twist, her taste mingling in. Just her lips made the animal inside him, the one dormant for so long, roar. It took all his strength to tone down the creature and move slowly. He pulled her closer, his arm snaking around her waist. She muffled a whimper against his lips. It only drove him to want more. He traced the crease in her lips with his tongue, pushing just the slightest to gain entry and when he prodded a break in them, he plunged in, exploring. He felt her tremble in his arms and that made him pause in pushing for more. The kiss alone was deep, and she was so delicious.

She mewled, her body curved against his. Her breasts were smashed against his chest, the apex of her thighs straddled the growing erection. Phineas experienced a rush of fire that made him scoop her up and take her to the bed. She said nothing but showered tiny kisses on his neck. He should put her down and go tend to the horses instead, but the heat of his loins stopped that idea. As he put her down next to the bed, he pulled back and looked at her.

"I so want to show you how truly beautiful you are."

Her lips were slightly swollen from his kisses, her eyes wide and dark. It was clear she was toying with this idea and if anything, that should have made him retreat, but it didn't. How many women had he known who took everything, always hoping for marriage or something, neither did they get. He had the reputation of a monk, at this point, because after a couple of near things being forced to the altar, he'd closed himself off. No Season. No courting. No wife. He always thought his betrothed's death was a blessing, more than not, for she'd been tied to him through their father's agreement, one the former Marquis of Huntington shoved down his throat. The girl, though, had had a tendre for another and went far to prove her love, in an attempt to thwart this arrangement, but it hadn't worked. No, instead she'd fallen ill…

His thoughts were interrupted by the modern Aphrodite in his arms when she ripped her lips from his.

"We can't do this," she pleaded, her voice husky, still trembling in his arms.

"No, we can't," he whispered back, then kissed her on her neck, his teeth slightly skating down from her ear. He knew he'd won as her head flung back and she moaned. He nipped at her shoulder. "I won't make love to you, but I can show you how marvelous life can be." And he grazed her shoulder line to her neck and let his tongue trace down her front to the top of the fiche. He glanced at her with a lopsided grin as he let his fingers trace under the dress's neckline.

Seduction didn't always mean fornication, and it'd take all he had to not to forget that.

Marina's head began to throb ever so slightly as her heart raced. Her body was unraveling it seemed. Inside, she was melting into molten lava, her lower belly tight and begging, but for what she didn't know. Him. That was obvious but…

That grin was wicked and the marquis, who had been so cold, almost avoiding the crowd of guests, now was entertaining her in ways she doubted were good. His kisses were addicting, and she wanted more. He was a flavor of wine, leather and man all wrapped into one sinful treat. But when he grated her neck and nipped lightly, she truly believed she'd turn into a puddle of liquid. Even now, as his fingers dipped lower, she knew she should object but her voice and sensible thinking fled.

Then he did the unthinkable. He managed to free her breasts from the top of the gown and gentle kissed her pert nipple, sending the tingles that blossomed there on an electric path inside her. He nibbled on her tip and sent a wave of excitement through her. Then he gave the other one equal attention. She was on fire and he seemed to be the only water left to stop it.

Her body craved more, and she found herself leaning against him, her hips matched to his. It was as if she had no control, and all turned slightly blurred, so she blamed the wine and his intoxicating kisses. And the snow, a voice deep inside her echoed.

Suddenly, she wanted to touch him, to return the

upending feeling that was consuming her. She put her hands on his shoulders and then wrapped her arms around his neck, her fingers weaving through his hair. When she was a child and got a new gift, the immediate need to see it all, to touch and play—the marquis made her feel all of that and more. She surprised herself as her desire turned her kisses to ferocious with a need she couldn't truly grasp, unlike anything she'd ever felt, and he met her with the same fervor.

She fell backward, slowly lowered by him, to the bed. Hungry, she moved her touch now down his chest, feeling the rock-hard muscles she hadn't expected from a gentleman. Intrigued, she measured down his side to his narrow waist and flat stomach. The bulge below that nestled against her at times, called for her to touch it and as she moved toward it, he switched positions, now next to her, to avoid it.

"No, my lady. To go that far would demand banns," he whispered hurriedly into her ear before his own hand traced down her middle and to her hip. He cupped the apex of her thighs, the area that was steaming with desire. Her nether lips were oddly throbbing, thick and swollen with need. He rocked her there, his thumb finding a sweet spot that made her quiver. The pace quickened but not fast enough for her. She mewled, wanting that release as the pressure climbed and they both rocked, his stroking increasing until everything in her mind exploded into a million stars. Her body arched, pressing against his hand, his thumb still twitching against her sweet spot that made her tremble for a few seconds.

As her body cooled and her thinking returned, she opened her eyes to find him next to her, another wicked grin on his face. She returned the smile and then shuddered.

He had ruined her without taking her virtue. *Oh, my*....

Chapter Nine

MARINA STIRRED, SUDDENLY CHILLED AND with the odd sensation of something slightly fuzzy brushing along her arm. The feeling didn't vanish, so she peered, barely opening her eyelids and found the fox, sniffing the sheet near her arm, her little whiskers skating along her flesh. When the animal took notice of her being awake, she chirped a high pitch noise, and scurried off. Marina frowned. Why did she leave? Marina had done nothing…

Finally opening her eyes, she re-oriented herself. She was on the bed, fully clothed, the blanket tucked nicely around her, and the marquis was nowhere to be found inside this tiny cottage. The cold, she discovered, developed as the fire in the hearth was down to embers.

What had happened last night?

She searched hard before the memories started to eke back to her. First was the hunt that fell into disarray when the skies thundered, and the rain turned to snow. And how her horse frightened, throwing her off and she did recall the fall ending abruptly. Even now, she touched the back of her scalp and found, on top of her fingers freezing, exposed to the room's temperature, that there was a knot, close to her neck and it was sore.

She swung her legs over the side of the bed and found her boots were on, though she didn't recall putting them on. Images of her dressed in her undergarments flooded her head, and the blanket she covered herself with, because he told her the dress was damp. A quick glance down told her it must have dried because it was on her now. Wine glasses on the table, with an empty bottle nearby told her the rest. They'd had a glass or two, he seduced her then gave her more wine. She must have collapsed on the bed. But memories of that euphoric moment in his arms stole her breath. He'd taken her to the stars. She sighed. Then shifted, moving her hip. Nothing hurt, like she'd heard it would when her virginity was taken. So he didn't take it?

It didn't matter if she was chaste or not. She'd spent the night in his company—that was enough to ruin her. Last night, that wasn't as awful sounding, for the wine after the bed play had been joyful. She learned about his sister and her tendre for Ewan, Viscount Featherton, and how Phineas' parents had died when he and Anne were too young, but he had to forge ahead, fast, to be able to take over the mantel of marquis, despite the lawyers who could handle the affairs till he was of age. And she had shared parts of her life, as a single child, whose mother had died in the childbirth bed. She managed to leave the possible marriage to Goodwood out, hoping that albatross was lifted.

But this morning, now, anger started to roll through her. Last night's episode with the marquis was a dream, she decided. The problem she saw was now, she was alone, in a gardener's cottage, far back on the estate and it'd snowed heavily…

So where was he?

The door burst open. A blast of cold blew in, right as the marquis entered, dressed in an overcoat and covered with snow.

"Marina, come. It is time for us to depart," he barked, handing her her cloak and bonnet.

She stared at him. "Good morning to you as well." She paused as he mussed around the room. "I daresay, have you no manners, my lord?"

He appeared to be in a great rush, but he stopped and gazed at her. She noticed his eyes were hard, his jawline set. "The snow has tapered, allowing us enough time to get out of here before it starts again. We need to get you back."

His tone irritated her. It was like he was another man, all business and no tender thoughts to a woman he had been intimate with the night before.

"I see." She jammed her bonnet on her head and bit back the wince when the back brim hit the swollen lump. That only increased her foul mood. "You take advantage of the situation last night, and today, fail to do what you must."

"It is because of that issue that we must leave now."

She peered out the iced over window. "It's barely dawn."

"Precisely," he stated, pouring the rest of the pitcher of water over the fire. "If we take it carefully, we should be back before the servants stir." He pulled the blanket off the bed. "Unless your wound hurts too much to travel?"

She was hurt and grateful, all at the same time. If it was safe to go, and they made it back before anyone noticed, all was well. But at the same point, she was hurt he could just shun her that way. But the frantic look in his eyes told her time was of the essence.

"No, I feel well enough to travel."

"Then, my lady, after you," he bowed, blanket in hand, as he motioned her out the door.

Saddled and wrapped again, Marina bit her bottom lip as they started down the snowy path. She glanced back at the cottage, trying to memorize the place in her head. Her heart thudded a slow and painful beat. She realized, in the time she'd spent with Phineas, he had stolen more than her innocence. He had stolen her heart.

The ride in the pre-dawn cold, across the pristine white snow-covered fields was as cold and silent as the winter was. He saw the anger in her eyes. Yes, he had leapt out of the bed when he woke. And it truly was a leap, because he had done the unthinkable again. In saving her, he had condemned them both in a society that would label her as ruined and his reputation would be in shambles if he didn't marry her.

But after Hester's death, he wanted no legal entanglements with women again. Privately, he'd sworn he'd not marry and so far, he'd been successful. His mistake with Marina was simply, she was a beautiful lady and he desired her in a way he had never wanted another. With a slow, careful seduction, he'd shown her the beauty of mating, but curbed his own heated desire to bury himself in her.

It had taken half a bottle of wine to drown the fire in his loins. Curling up with her in the bed, both dressed, her under the cover and him on top, also caused friction, as his erection returned but he'd managed, despite the pain. Wine had helped, again.

But this morning? He raced out to see the snow had tapered. It'd drifted so it wasn't entirely thick everywhere and the horses, under a lean-to he'd designed last summer when he came during the rains, had rested and were twitching to leave as well.

So when he came to get Marina, her quick anger surprised him. He had no time to figure it out, making him appear cold and indifferent. Perhaps, he was, except he discovered he really started to be pulled to her.

Pushing that deep thought aside, he guided them through the woods and smiled. Over his shoulder, he announced, "And we are here."

She said nothing but then again, she was probably chilled. He nudged his horse to pick up the pace and her mare followed suit. They got to the back side of the house, near the stables. He dismounted and then lifted her off her saddle. When his hands gripped her waist, a whirlwind of memories and heat flared inside him. He knew she felt it too, from the look in her grey eyes. Eyes that took on the deep hue of purple when she was giving in to the ecstasy that he created in her.

Stop that!

Giving her a silent nod, he unsaddled the horses in record time, and slapped their hindquarters, giving them the cue to race to their stalls and he threw hay in. When he got back to Marina, she was shivering. He took her hand and raced to the house, using his library door to enter.

The house was dark, only a faint clattering of pans in the kitchen to be heard.

"Go to your room. Hopefully your cousin sleeps soundly." He kissed her lips. The act was automatic, and it caught him off guard, which he didn't like, but there was no time now to think.

"Of course. Good night, Lord Rockford." And with her skirt gathered in her arm, she ran up the steps.

He threw his coat to the armchair and went to the cabinet. Yanking his best bottle of brandy, he poured a healthy portion, downing it in one gulp. Still considering that, the door flew wide open. He frowned.

"Why, Lady Margaret, good morning to you. Bit early, don't you think?" He finally downed a gulp. The elder aunt was one of the few he trusted to watch over his sister and she had been very diligent as her chaperone. Watching over him, though, was another matter...

But Margaret Kimball's face held nothing warm. "You have a problem, my lord."

How the hell had she discovered Marina and his little secret? Did she see them ride in? Margaret was never an early riser.

"Dear Auntie, surely you just woke too early. The snow is quite lovely," he added and thought that was asinine. He poured another glass with a moderate portion. "Here."

She didn't take it but just glared at him. "Anne

is missing."

His fist tightened around the glass. He swore he'd throw his sister into a convent and strangle Featherton!

Suddenly, Marina appeared behind his aunt. "My cousin, Lady Ruth, isn't here!"

"Hinds!" he bellowed down the hall. He didn't care if no one was up.

His butler appeared. "Yes, my lord."

"Have you seen Lady Anne or Lady Ruth?"

"No sir."

Phineas' blood started to boil. "And what of Viscount Featherton?"

Hinds didn't move an inch. "No sir. Nor the Earl of Riverbend."

His hands clenched into fists and it took a concerted effort to uncurl his fingers. "Did everyone else return from the hunt?"

"Yes, sir," Hinds replied. "Not all at once but straggled in. The snow, sir."

He knew about the damn snow! He gritted his teeth. If all were accounted for, he did find it oddly interesting that the man didn't include Phineas and Marina in that account. He pushed that thought aside and returned to now.

Riverbend and Featherton ran off with Lady Ruth and Anne? He shook the thought of Riverbend and Lady Ruth. "Has the house been searched?"

Margaret piped right in. "Of course, it has. We've turned every handle, searched every pantry."

"Hinds, have the stables checked."

"Yes, my lord."

Phineas yanked at his neckcloth. What the hell

was Anne doing?

Hinds returned. "My lord, the stables are in an uproar. It appears the black carriage is not here nor is the team matched for it."

"Oh, dear heavens!" Margaret cried. "They've run to Gretna Green!"

Chapter Ten

MARINA HEARD THE ELDER LADY shriek and swore her shrill tongue set Marina's ears to ringing. Gretna Green? She blinked. Didn't she know what that was? The dull thud in the back of her head now seemed to moved to her temples or was it in between her eyes? Her vision seemed to blur or was that her thinking? Way too much was happening. She'd worried her night of indiscretion would ruin her, that his refusal to make the situation right angered and upset her and why hadn't anyone commented on their late return or the sudden appearance of their horses or why they were both dressed as they had been the day before? But her answer swirled before her. Phineas face reflected his anger toward the situation of his sister, his jaw tightly set, the close-set brows bunching. And Lady Margaret had the servants going in a whirlwind to try to right the upset in Rockford Hall.

For some reason, she knew she should join in the mayhem, side with Phineas or Lady Margaret, both who feared an unplanned and unapproved union, but the truth was, she was furious that she was thrown aside, as it were, like wash water. Disgusted, she started to turn, to return to her room and finally wash away last night in the washbowl when her Aunt Clare ran down the stairs and straight toward her.

"Marina, darling, I can't find your cousin."

It was Ruth's fault she was here, Marina decided. Though the invitation had come to her, Marina's despondent mood simply tossed it aside after her father mentioned his intention for her to wed the shipper sow, Ruth had impressed how this event might save her such a demise. It had disrupted her dark winter but the loss of her innocence, with or without her maidenhead, marred her to the point of a scarlet mark on her soul. The fact that even her aunt worried more about her cousin simply set her inner teapot to boil.

"According to the staff and guests," she stated. "You won't. She ran off to Gretna Green with a few others."

"What!?"

"I believe I spoke plainly enough," she stifled a yawn and moved up the stairs.

As she drudged up the stairs, she heard the pitter-patter of feet descending and heard her Aunt Clare adding to the chaos about Ruth missing, which set Lady Margaret into another uproar. Vaguely, as she turned the corner in the hall, she heard Phineas order all the servants to the kitchen, his aunt and Aunt Clare to the dining room and told them he'd be there shortly. By the time she reached her door, all was subdued below.

Sliding inside her room, she closed the door and slumped against it. A whirlwind of emotions swirled inside her head and heart, making it difficult to think. She'd spent the night in the arms, as it were, of a man who stole her heart and she'd allowed herself to think maybe, he might have some feelings for her. But as the dawn peeked, she came to the realization that last night's intimacy and the talk and laughter afterwards over the wine held no lingering effects on him today. They'd shared a great deal and yet, nothing. One thing was certain, she decided. While she had no idea what had happened to Phineas' previous betrothal, the woman had died and her death had marred him badly, to the point, apparently, of not wanting to consider marriage again. Or, at least, any time soon.

Anger quickly replaced her melancholy, and she pushed off the door, heading straight for the water pitcher and bowl. She grabbed the linen, doused it and vigorously scrubbed her face, neckline and arms, rubbing so hard her skin prickled and she saw it turn red. That only built her irritability higher. She splashed water on her face and neck, determined to cool and wash the soap away. As she placed the dry linen on her face to dry, she heard a noise, so paused.

"Marina, why are you not downstairs, helping us fined your cousin?"

Marina closed her eyes, counting to herself. "I needed to clean up, Aunt Clare."

"Harrumph!"

Slowly, Marina watched her aunt through the looking glass above the washbowl, as her aunt walked over to the bed and lifted the skirt of her riding habit.

"You've ruined this dress, Marina." The woman snorted, dropping the material.

Of course, her aunt had always favored Ruth. That had been obvious for years. Marina had been hurt by the favoritism as a child until she overheard her father and Aunt Clare in a heated discussion one afternoon. Ruth's mother was Aunt Clare's sister, as had been Marina's. Apparently, Aunt Clare believed Ruth's father was of a better quality than Marina's father was. She learned in that one afternoon, Aunt Clare believed the Earl of Lockhart killed his wife, forcing her delicate body to give him an heir. Marina's world flipped at that remark and even more so when the earl turned on his sister-in-law she was nothing more than jealous of her sister for marrying him.

Ever since then, Marina tolerated her aunt, gave her the respect needed as an elder, but inside, she saw her exactly as her father penned her. A woman angered over a lost love. So Aunt Clare's affection toward Ruth made sense. It did not mean Marina did not love her cousin but now, the fact her aunt made no comment about *her* absence, just that she ruined *her* dress and not herself, disturbed her no end.

"My mare frightened during the hunt, spun too fast and she threw me."

"Well, the riding habit you'll rarely need, and perhaps Dottie can work on it," her aunt muttered. Then she looked at Marina. "You appear well?"

Marina fought the feeling of warmth that invaded her bones. Aunt Clare was only asking so later she could claim she cared. "I have a minor knot on my head, but other than that nuisance, I am fine."

The woman scurried over. "Let me see."

"No, truly, it is fine." Why had she ever said anything? Perhaps, she needed to feel someone cared, even if it was only temporary. So she sat still as

Aunt Clare tipped her head, looking for a visible mark. "It was a bump on the side. It is better this morning."

"Well," her aunt huffed, stepping back. "If you're health has improved, let us descend and help find your hostess and cousin. Come along."

Aunt Clare grabbed her shawl tighter and left. Marina stood and with a deep sigh, resigned herself to her own fate. Picking up her own wrap, she ambled down the stairs and tried her best to ignore the tug at her heart that would go unheard.

Chapter Eleven

PHINEAS PACED. GRETNA GREEN. IF Viscount Featherton thought for one second he could take the Marquis of Rockford's sister off to exchange vows without proper banns, he'd skin the man alive!

He glanced out the window again. He had the stable boys out, to see if they could find the carriage tracks and their direction. In the snow, that should be an easy task. He needed time to think and let his favorite mount rest and recover from the weather conditions. Horses ate hay to keep themselves warm in the chill of winter, eating more than in the warmer months, but he hadn't been able to scour as much as needed to keep them munching as much as Phineas thought was needed. They both appeared to fare well but saddling Star and going galloping off to beat Ewan to shreds for this didn't seem advisable right away. The stallion's health was important, especially in this temperature. But damn!

Lady Margaret sat on the settee, tapping her foot, her shoulders square and the look of impatience clear on her face. "You need to find her! And her friend!"

Phineas' gaze narrowed. "I will, rest assure on that."

Suddenly, Lady Clare and Lady Marina rushed into the room.

"Well? Have they been found?" The elder lady demanded.

Phineas rolled his eyes upward, but he could feel the heat of Marina, as if she aimed it right at him. He gave her a look and she quickly diverted hers. That puzzled him, because she stood there, glowing a delightful light from a night of discovering how beautiful another could make her feel and for that initiation, she avoided him.

"He's waiting for reports, my dear," Lady Margaret replied.

"Waiting for reports?" The woman shrieked.

Phineas spun on his heels and opened his mouth to quiet the woman when his head stable boy appeared at the door.

"Yes, lad, do tell." He motioned the boy in.

"Sir, we lost the carriage tracks past the drive. Snow, sir. It must've covered it." The boy twisted his hat in his hands as he spoke.

Phineas' jaw tightened. "And any horse tracks?"

"Buried, my lord."

"Get Star saddled…"

"And Lilly," a feminine voice added.

Phineas turned. Marina was glaring at him, the demand to go a fury sounding in her simple words. Well, it was her cousin among the missing…

"Yes, saddle Lilly as well."

The boy nodded and nearly ran into the doorframe in his desperate speed to leave. Phineas looked at her. She was beautiful, all lit with fire with determination. He found himself giving her a half grin.

The elder ladies, though, immediately jumped in, demanding she not put herself in peril and accusing him of allowing her to be put in danger's path. Inwardly, he laughed. If they had any idea just how far he had led her…

He walked to the doorway and stood, waiting for Marina. The chaperones followed in tow, still ranting how it was not ladylike to go on search parties.

"Ladies, please," Phineas finally interrupted. "It is quite clear Lady Marina is worried about her cousin and is more than capable to come with me to search."

"Not only is it unladylike," Lady Margaret argued. "But highly inappropriate for a lady to ride with a bachelor, even here in the countryside."

"So, Lady Margaret, would you like me to have a mare saddled for you as well?" He couldn't resist the jab, for he knew the answer.

"Good heavens, how could you think that! I am a lady!"

"So is Lady Marina. But she has concerns and I welcome her company, so let her go in peace." He turned to his butler, who held his wool coat, gloves and hat. As he started to put them on, the door banged open and a rush of cold air flooded the entryway.

"We've been out, scouring the countryside, looking for bodies, to find you're here! Simply marvelous!" Ewan spouted, yanking his snow-flaked wool cloak off and handing his damp leather gloves and hat to the servant.

"Oh, brother, you had us all in fits, not making it home!" Anne let the servant take her cloak, hat and gloves. She eyed her brother, her gaze narrowing. "How long have you been home?"

Spilling in behind them was Ruth and Riverbend. All four looked cold, tired but in good spirits. Ruth rushed over to her cousin, taking her hands and giving her cheeks a kiss.

"I was so worried, Marina."

Marina gave her a smile. "You're freezing. Come, into the library. There is a fire going."

"I saw you take that fall," Ruth continued as they headed into the large room. "Oh, my, yes, it is warm in here." She raced to the fireplace, careful not to get too close, and put her hands out to pick up the heat.

"Yes." Anne was next into the room. She went to the large leather chair near the fireplace. "It had turned wicked out there. Several of our horses seemed to spook, as they will. One goes mad, they all follow suit—"

"They do not 'go mad', sister," Phineas corrected. "Just the unusual weather set them off. It does not thunder and snow at the same time, so to speak."

"Nevertheless," Anne continued, brushing Phineas off as she turned toward Marina. "Ewan saw you fall, but you were not close, and he saw my brother nearby, so he grabbed my reins and said we'd better hurry to the house."

"That is true," Ewan agreed. "Snows like this can be heavy and fast." He snorted. "You look rather out of sorts, Rockford."

Phineas frowned. "I don't understand." He poured them all brandy. "Here, this should rid you of the rest of the chill." He handed a glass to his sister and then turned to see Marina trying to warm

Ruth's hands. She seemed to be avoiding his gaze.

"Yes, I dare say, my good man," Riverbend said. "Isn't that the same jacket you wore on the hunt?"

Phineas stiffened, his hands wanting to curl into fists, but he held a brandy snifter. He took a sip and felt the warmth seep into him as it traveled down his throat. "I dare say, we all seem to be close to the same." Heavens, he never noticed what men wore, and little of the ladies. For the ladies, he usually found himself undressing them over memorizing what they wore.

Marina shot him a quick glance from over the rim of her glass. Prodding his memory, he guessed Riverbend was right. He seemed to recall taking that dress off her and how intricate the ties were… The memory of undressing her of the riding habit made him want to smile, as he glanced at Marina over his own glass.

Out of the corner of his eye, he caught Anne and Ewan watching him and then exchanging a knowing look between them.

"So, dearest brother," Anne started, setting her brandy snifter down. "What time did you two make it home? Surely before the snow drifted…."

Phineas guffawed, as if caught off guard so he coughed to cover the mistake. "I went looking for Lady Marina. I found her horse, riderless, and in a clearing. But no signs of the lady. I feared she'd been thrown, so I started to hunt for her." He swallowed, trying to drown the memory of her mewl as he got her to climax. "Took hours but I did find her, safe and sound, in the gardener's cottage."

Anne's eyebrows shot up. "Truly? And how did she find that?"

"I'm sure she found it after she fell and found herself alone, as we all had left. So I escorted her back to the house." It was such a lie, but he wasn't about to ruin the lady's reputation by the truth.

"She stayed the night, alone, in a cottage in the woods? In the cold?" Ewan asked, his tone equally shocked.

"Well, the cottage is well stocked with blankets and such. If you'll notice, she is fine." He smiled at her and hoped she'd not call him a liar.

They all turned and looked at her.

Marina sat, totally mortified and shocked. All hopes that the sow her father wanted her to marry had vanished with a marquis making right his ruining of her went flying out the front door, freezing into nothing. She'd crawled to a cottage on her own, started a fire, ate and slept until help came? Was he really thinking they'd believe that?

The truth blind-sided her. He didn't want her. She gulped, her shoulders still steeled but her lips pursed, like they did before she lost her ladylike appearance, but she managed to refrain from roasting him over the fire in the hearth. She could tell the truth, lose her virtue and all chance at finding true love, forced to marry a marquis who obviously did not want her. It took every ounce of energy she had not to slump in despair, or worse, run to her room.

She put on the mask she wore around her father, when he called on her for something he'd blame her for. It was as blank a look as she could muster.

Then she added a curt smile.

"My mare frightened by the thunder and I fell, and hit my head on a log, I believe. Made me dizzy so I managed to stumble, holding onto a stick I found, looking for the path back but it was snowing hard." She adjusted her shoulders. "I was afraid I was lost and turned to find a quaint little shack." Her gaze fell on the marquis. "What a lovely surprise to find a shelter when I was in need. There were plenty of blankets and some tea and biscuits I could dine on, waiting for the storm to stop or someone to find me. And the marquis did. My guardian angel was watching over me."

When she stopped, her aunt, along with Anne, Ruth and Margaret, raced to her, questions on her injury raging in front of her while she kept a silent conversation with the marquis. The message she sent him was she had saved him. But not again.

Chapter Twelve

PHINEAS WAITED UNTIL MARINA, HER cousin and aunt, and the rest of the party retired before he sent for his sister and Ewan. He poked the fire again, trying to cool the fury that blazed inside him. They had some explaining to do.

But his major point of concern, the one he kept shoving to the back of his mind, was Marina. Anne argued they had taken off in a snowstorm to find the lady they had witnessed fall. Their turning the cards on him, asking him where he had been, had caught him off guard, something he rarely had happen. It had pushed him into a corner, and instead of being truthful, telling them he had rescued her to start with and kept her safe till travel was better, the words that fell from his mouth painted a lovely picture that kept him out of wedlock and Marina with survival instincts she didn't know she had, nor that any lady of her station possessed. He saw the flash of emotions in Marina's gaze, just as he'd seen the light in her eyes when she shattered beneath his seduction. He had to make it up to her, though he wasn't sure how. The only solution was marriage and that he refused to do. Not until it was truly forced on him!

Of course, Lady Marina could indeed let everyone know she'd spent the night with him and all bets were off, as the church bells would be ringing....

"You called, brother?"

He glanced up and found the culprits at the door. "Do come in."

Anne glided into the room, followed by Ewan. Viscount Featherton was all eyes for the Lady Anne but he kept a safe distance and sat on the settee with her but not next to her.

Phineas leaned against his desk, facing them. "Quite a fascinating tale of your search for Lady Marina. I must commend you."

Anne flattened her skirts, her lips pursed. Ewan didn't move.

"It was the truth, Phin. Lord Riverbend pulled his spirited animal under control and caught a glimpse of Lady Marina's tumble."

"So your first thought was to race back to the house, grab a carriage to take out into a snowstorm?" He worked hard to keep his tone pleasant, but his anger was still boiling.

"Surely, you didn't mean we should've left her to her own devices," Ewan added.

"Of course not. Don't be daft. But that carriage would not be of much help in a rescue."

He carefully watched them, to see their response to that statement.

"It was the only equipage ready to go," Anne replied. "The horses were fresh."

"And the snow was piling up," Ewan finished.

Phineas pinched the bridge of his nose as he closed his eyes. "It was also the right vehicle, in better weather, to ride north in, to say, Gretna Green."

Anne straightened, her cheeks pinked. Ewan

looked like he was fighting a grin.

"Was that your true plan?" he prodded.

"What if it was?" Anne pounced. "We didn't, of course, nor would we, for we have played by your rules this week."

Ewan took her hand and put it in the crux of his arm as he looked at his friend. "Rockford, I love her, and she loves me. But running to Gretna in this weather was unwise, and I will not risk my darling Anne in such a manner." He tilted his head to look at his lady as he squeezed her hand.

She smiled and blushed. Phineas shook his head.

"So, you will refrain from eloping until we can discuss this clearly? *After* the holidays," he demanded softly. He sighed. "Anne, I'd rather you have a season before settling."

She got up and hugged him. "I will take the season, but it will not change my heart."

"You, then, are a silly gel." He shook his head.

"My friend, not all women are like Lady Montberry. You yourself, need to move forward. You need an heir and a spare, if you'll recall," Ewan prodded, though his smile was for Anne.

The sound of her name made him cringe. "No, there will not be another Hester…"

"Grand! What of Lady Marina?"

He frowned at his sister. "Lady Marina has other engagements on her plate."

"So order another set!" Ewan laughed.

Phineas could hardly contain a snarl. He'd never put himself in that place again. But he was so caught in his disgust, he didn't see till too late, Anne was at his side, her eyes tinged with excitement. She kissed his cheek.

"Lady Marina could be yours. All you have to do is ask." She gave him another kiss. "Good night, brother."

He watched them whisk out of the room. *Ask?* They were mad—he swore, after Hester, he'd never trust a woman again!

Five days before Christmas...

MARINA INHALED AS THE MAID, Eve, pulled on her hair with the brush, then twisted the dark curls, pinning them to the back of her head. One of the pins hit the still sore spot from the accident and she winced.

"Sorry, my lady."

"It's all right." Marina held still, tight as a drum, waiting for another stab that didn't come.

"Oh, that's marvelous! Please do mine, Eve," Ruth called.

The maid pulled two more ringlet curls at the base of her hair, clucking softly. "There. Do you like it, my lady?"

Marina glanced into the looking glass. It was stunning, like one of the paintings of Ancient Greece, with her curls piled high, hemmed in by ivory topped combs, a halo of curls that escaped, giving her a soft look. She tipped her head. The headaches had stopped and sleeping on her back was slowly possible, that was if she could keep from being poked there. Even so, she looked young and naïve. That was a jest, never to be answered.

The door opened slightly and one of the other

maids entered. She came right to Marina with a note in her hand.

"Delivered for Lady Lockhart."

Marina took it and split the seal. The contents made her stomach flip. She shut her eyes, praying what it said wasn't true.

Ruth, facing the looking glass, gave her a puzzled look. "Cousin, what's wrong?"

Marina inhaled and bit her bottom lip. "Nothing of concern." She slid the note onto the bureau and swallowing her dismay, she walked over to her cousin. Ruth smiled.

"We will be the belles of the ball tonight, I think."

Marina returned the grin. "You will be, that is certain."

As Eve stepped aside, Ruth turned and took Marina's hands. "There is still a chance for you to escape that cloud you've been standing under."

"Cloud?" She'd been disappointed that Phineas had lied about them and avoided the ladies, she was sure because of her, the last day and a half.

"Yes," Ruth nodded. "The one that has made you so quiet and sad looking. Even more so now. What did the note say?"

Sad? She'd thought mad, but in respective, sad was probably correct.

"It is nothing for you to worry about," she replied. "I am fine."

The puzzled frown on Ruth's face intensified but then vanished, as if she accepted her cousin's false statement that she was fine. Eve brought out the gowns. "Oh, Marina, of course tonight will be grand! It's the Christmas ball!" She leaned forward, dropping her voice. "Who knows what we might get as gifts. Perhaps a handsome lord!"

Marina couldn't help but laugh. "And what would you do with a lord, if given one?"

"One to marry, of course!"

Marry. That brought a frown that she fought desperately to stop. "Not all are worth marriage." Her thoughts still whirling over the marquis and her note.

"Oh, Marina, there's that cloud again! *Shish, shish*!" She waved away the imaginary cloud. "Think happy thoughts. Perhaps the Marquis of Rockford will whisk you away and make you his marchioness!"

With a pasted smile, she hugged her cousin. If life was only that easy. "Merry Christmas, Ruth."

"Early Merry Christmas to you, too. It's still a few days away." Ruth hugged her back.

Marina sat and watched her cousin get dressed, her excitement spilling over the room, even onto Marina. She decided she'd have fun tonight, because tomorrow, she'd be going home. Back to be tied to Lord Goodwood.

How she so wanted to scream.

Ruth knew her cousin too well. Something had happened on the hunt. The heat between her and the marquis was palatable – everyone noticed it, but no one, not even Anne, said a word to either of them. Yet that letter Marina had received made her cousin's black cloud now a thunderstorm from the look on her face. Since her cousin refused to tell her, Ruth waited until they were to go to the ball and then insisted she'd forgotten her fan. She raced back to the room and went to the bureau, rummaging for the slip of paper.

She found it. It was from the Earl of Lockhart, Marina's father. Ruth flipped it over and opened it at the broken seal.

My dearest daughter,

It is imperative that you leave for home on the morrow. I know it is before your holiday party is through, but our plans have changed. Lord Goodwood will take you for wife now, which should please you, getting a husband for the holiday.

I'll expect your arrival shortly.
Merry Christmas, with love,
Lockhart

Ruth's mouth dropped open. That evil man had moved her nuptials to now? With no chance at the Season? No chance to find a happier match? She folded the note, sliding it back to where she found it, her gaze narrowing.

She'd have to talk to Anne. Left to her, Marina would not disobey her father, who couldn't even sign the note with endearment of Father. Despicable man, she thought. Tapping her jawline, Ruth came to a solution and smiled, assured Anne would help. She raced off to the ball, determined to save her cousin.

Chapter Thirteen

THE BALL REIGNED AS THE highlight of the house party. Phineas gave a heavy sigh, leaning against the balcony pillar, overlooking the ballroom floor, a brandy snifter in his hand. This was the final big event for this week of festivities and after tomorrow, all these guests would be gone, and he'd have his house back to himself. Downing another gulp of the pirated brandy, letting it burn a clear path down his throat, he let his thoughts ponder that idea, of the estate back to just him and Anne. It was a marvelous and disastrous idea. Anne would no doubt drive him to murder, badgering him in Ewan's defense. But, if memory served, he did tell them it was possible, though she still got her Season and he'd pray to all heaven above she'd find another…

Then there was the other issue. Marina. He found her in his thoughts more and more and that troubled him. The fact that he had an intimate moment with her was incriminating. Yet truth was, he had been attracted to her on the first day he'd met her, in the library. She was a raven-haired beauty. Her gray eyes brought him in closer, for he'd never seen that color and it glimmered different shades, reflecting her mood, he decided. Her response to his touch set off a fire that still burned deep within him. The recognition of that desire made him tug at his collar, suddenly tight. *Could he just let her go?*

"You intend to simply hide up here all night?"

He didn't turn. It was Riverbend. "I wager Anne sent you?"

Riverbend laughed. "Who would I be, if not a gentleman, to oblige a lady?"

Phineas snorted and turned to see his friend, who, for once, didn't look like he'd just awoken and put on the closest clothes to hand. Riverbend was an original, he mused, for most of the *ton*, including the men, dressed as Brummel ordained, but not Riverbend. The Earl of Riverbend never cared and in fact, rubbed it in Brummel's face that a lord was fine with messy hairstyles, slightly wrinkled shirts and waistcoats and boots that didn't shine. But tonight, his attire was perfect for a ball, despite his hair and the cowlick that refused to stay in place, pomade or not.

"And what did Lady Anne require?"

"Well, considering you're the host, that you and she start the promenade." He grinned.

Of course, the beginning march, done to music that flowed like a dance, so they could all weave around the room, to basically see what everyone wore. Utterly ridiculous with this group, since they'd been mingling on the floor for the past hour. Yet, Anne wanted perfection. It was Christmas. He downed the rest of his brandy.

"Let us not keep the lady waiting."

Marina managed to keep the smile on her face,

despite the nagging note that ruined her mood. She was determined to make this night magical, because her Season was cut off before it began. Soon, she'd be Lady Goodsow, no, she corrected, Lady Goodwood, and allow him the privileges marriage gave him. The mere suggestion of that brought the memory of her evening with the marquis slamming back into her thoughts, of his gentle, seductive caress, his darkened blue eyes and those lips that took her to heaven, not to mention what his fingers did to her below…

The recall sent a tingle through her body, one that shot straight down her spine to her lower abdomen and the core beneath, where a flame ignited. She shifted on her feet, vaguely listening to Lord Hornshow ramble about something, and became acutely aware how she felt damp between her thighs, just like she had when Phineas touched her. She swallowed the lump in her throat and tried to cool the fire by finishing her champagne.

After the promenade, the music started. Everyone danced. Everyone but the marquis. She saw he stood to the side, usually in deep conversation with one of the lords, but she never caught a glance her way from him. She couldn't stop the wave of loss, that he no longer desired her company after he'd ruined her in that night, a night she could never tell a soul about without it making him a liar. He'd be forced to marry her and she'd no doubt, they'd spend their lives miserable, because he'd never forgive her.

She spun and ran right into the Earl of Riverbend. "Oh, pardon me. I didn't see you."

The tall, blond lord gazed down his crooked nose

and smiled. "It should be pardon me, my lady, for I just came to ask if you'd like to dance?"

Surprised, her eyes widened as she stuttered, "That would be grand."

Riverbend bowed and took her offered hand and led her out onto the ballroom floor.

Phineas acted as nonchalant as he could. He truly didn't care if he was here, if he danced or even talked to another person but he did, for as host, he couldn't avoid it. Yet, he was talking to Smitherton, Lorrance and Hardin, who had just finished a round of dances and come to imbibe in some of his ill-gotten brandy. As their conversation turned towards the war, he managed to keep an eye on that luscious lady he'd sampled a taste of in the gardener's cottage. Of the lady who didn't condemn him for having a wild fox as a pet and even played with Petunia herself. Lady Marina was a mystery, for any others would have screamed, run out the door or scolded him for trying to tame a wild creature. That and she didn't flirt with him, which simply amused and baffled him. Every other lady did, so why didn't she?

The gentlemen around him started to laugh but he didn't hear the jest. He raised a brow, praying they weren't plotting how to seduce one of these ladies, or how to throw him out into the snow for interfering in Anne and Ewan's relationship.

Hardin was the first to speak. "Apologies, but how long does it take a lord to come out of mourning?"

"I never said I remained in mourning."

Another round of snickers passed amongst them.

"Are you sure, lad? Because we've yet to see you among the ladies on the dance floor," Hardin commented.

Phineas shot him an evil look. "You realize my aim here is to keep Anne safe."

"Safe from what?" Hardin countered. "None here would seek her harm. And Featherton adores her."

"It's precisely him I'm watching."

Hardin chuckled, his ginger looks making him appear jolly, one who never saw evil, even as it loomed over them. "Perhaps, you might realize she's watching over you, old man."

Phineas frowned. "Why?"

"You've been a fright since that ghastly drama with your bride to be."

"My lord, I'd be careful if I were you," he warned.

"Oh, do move on. She wronged you, and it was clearly evident to all involved. Her death was a travesty, but none of your doing." Hardin shook his head in disgust. "Lady Anne is more worried that you've been a recluse since and fears you wish to draw her into your trap of seclusion. Look, even now," he waved his arms about. "This estate is the furthest of your holdings, far from London, yet you hibernate here. 'Tis part of her reason for this house party, and," he leaned closer, his voice dropped, "hopes that one lady here would garner your attention."

"Poppycock," Phineas threw back the rest of his drink.

"If that be the truth," Hardin straightened. "Then come to the dance floor and prove her wrong."

"I'm hardly a dancer."

"Utter nonsense!" Hardin looked past Phineas, over the balcony railing to the dancers below. "Look, that pretty one that you helped save from the weather and wild horses is dancing with Cardemon. Hopefully, he won't step on her toes, or her dress!"

Phineas reluctantly glanced over the edge. It was true. Lord Winston Cardemon was traipsing on the dance floor with that angelic beauty, Marina. From here, she looked like she floated over the marble floor. That was, until Cardemon lost his footing and stumbled, only to regain himself, but he knocked into poor Marina and she had to side step to keep the train of her shimmering ivory silk dress from being anchored, and probably ripped, by Cardemon's fall. When the lord righted himself, laughed with her over his folly, he pulled her back to him and that movement, which looked way too close and tight, sending a shot of anger through Phineas. How dare that arse touch her so! She wasn't Cardemon's, by God!

Without another thought, he pushed Hardin aside and raced down the stairs, the echo of Hardin's laughter ringing in his ears. Phineas decided he'd box them later, but for now, he needed to save Marina from Cardemon's hands.

Marina allowed herself the luxury of the dance, of the steps and twirls required in the sets that mingled, separated to move into the next repetitive sequence of footsteps, all set to the sounds of the small string ensemble. By the candlelight and scent of evergreens, apples and cinnamon, the element of the holiday seeped into her bones and lifted her spirits, despite the clumsiness of her partner.

She'd come to the ball, her motivation to be part of the activity marred by her father's note. It had dampened her spirit, which had been damaged by the marquis, who had taken her to the heavens, and then quickly forgotten her, as if it never happened. Her solution to her situation was to dance and she quickly skirted across the dance floor for most of the evening. It was a festive time and she enjoyed it with only one thought nagging at her. Where was the marquis?

"Lady Marina," Cardemon said, as the dance finished and after he bowed to her. He offered his hand. "Shall we find some punch, to refresh you?"

She smiled. Cardemon was a true gentleman, well-mannered, well-dressed and, if she recalled correctly, of a very old lineage of good family. Of course, he'd be outstanding, being a friend of the marquis to be so invited, but it did not matter, because despite his family name and wealth, he'd never be good enough to ignore her lack of dowry and her father's insistence of the match he'd made for her. Right now, the tall, dark haired gentleman, with two left feet, had an infectious smile and a twinkle in his eye that bespoke of mischief-maker. She'd liked him within the first minute.

But he wasn't Phineas.

She sighed and took Cardemon's hand, so he might escort her to the punch table. There, they joined Ruth and the others.

"Enjoying yourself?" Ruth ribbed her softly.

Taking the cup from the servant behind the table, she nodded. "As much as I can, dear cousin."

"Good. Because the marquis is walking this way."

Marina nearly choked on her punch. He was here? Now? She hoped she looked presentable but now, she faltered. Concentrating, she worked to calm her heartbeat, which had taken off at an erratic pace at the mere suggestion he was here, yet where else would he be? This was his house and his house party!

"Good evening, ladies."

It was a soft greeting and the vibrations from it reverberated through her. She gulped.

"Good evening, Lord Rockford," she managed to squeak out. Ruth chimed in as well.

Phineas stood and had a grin on his face, jovial looking even, though his eyes looked intense as he stared at her. The rest of his body leaned, and in the black jacket, waistcoat and trousers, he looked handsome. A hunger started in her stomach and sank lower as a memory of his touch sent sparks to that area he shouldn't have touched and now, her body begged for it. She was speechless. Ruth rattled about the dancing and he answered but she had absolutely no clue what they said because her blood was pounding through her and the racket filled her ears with the thudding of her heart.

In the distance, the musicians started again. Out of the corner of her eye, Marina saw many of the men going to a lady to request the dance. Would the marquis ask her? She hoped so.

"Would you care to dance?"

She spun and found Anne's love, Lord Featherton, at her side, offering to take her hand. A frown threatened, and she fought against it. The fact Featherton was here surprised her. With Phineas here, an inner thread to her soul begged him to ask her to dance but the invitation never came so she took Featherton's offered hand and nodded.

Phineas watched but said nothing. Oh, she needed to forget him. She was already promised to another man…

He stood there, aghast, that his sister's admirer just took that beautiful lady away from him, like that! He blinked, his temper roused. His whole purpose in finally coming down from his perch above was to whisk her away onto the dance floor, using the only method available to hold her close that was appropriate. No, Featherton walked up and asked her before he could get the words out.

Well, two could play that game. Her cousin was already taking her spot on the dance floor with Frankworth. So he scanned the room and found his sister.

"Anne, dance with me."

Her brows rose as she smirked, putting her gloved hand in his. "That was hardly a proper invitation, brother."

He spun her on the dance floor, next to another couple and muttered, "We are related. Casualty is allowed."

The music started, and the couples curtsied and bowed before they started. It was the waltz, done in sets of four. This dance moved the couple dancing through sets with one couple, before the rhythm changed and they turned to dance with the next set.

"You look distracted, brother," Anne commented during the configuration that had them together.

He held a tight smile but couldn't stop the growl. His sister laughed. She was light on her feet and swayed easily, at ease in the dance. He, on the other hand, wasn't, though he knew the steps so well he doubted anyone noticed he was gauging the number of sets until they reached Marina and Featherstone. He glanced at Anne and muffled a snort when he saw her chin rise just a little, to look beyond the group they were with.

It took two more sets before he was opposite of Marina. She gave him a smile and its beauty melted the core of anger inside him. During the move that had them sway between each other and end up opposite, he managed to sneak out a line.

"You look divine."

She turned her head so fast, he feared she'd slip. When he came in to take her hand to swing her once before releasing, she managed to whisper, "Thank you, my lord."

That whisper circled down his ear, hit a cord that sent a fiery bolt down his spine to his loins and ignited his desires. Damn, he wanted her! It suddenly became a driving force, as if she was his siren and called for him. At the next steps that brought the four together, to put one hand in and join to dance a circle then split to turn and start with another couple, he grabbed her hand as they started to release, pulled her away.

He broke the line, taking her to the open part of the floor. Vaguely, he heard the small commotion and the looks as the dancing stopped, but not the music. The string quartet did falter but, as he was their employer and a lord, they continued the slow rhythm of the flowing tune.

Marina's gaze widened, a look of surprise and amusement playing across those grey eyes. His own lips curled, for he was pleased she appeared unworried. He was breaking the rules of society. He knew that. So did she, but she wasn't fleeing. As he stopped and turned her toward him, he put his right hand on her waist lightly and took her hand in his left, leaving fewer inches than the rulebook said. He caught his sister tightly shaking her head and Featherton along with Riverbend nodding at him, as if he'd won some contest.

"My lord?"

He glanced down. They were set to start but he'd stopped. "Apologies," he whispered. "Shall we dance, Lady Marina?"

At her nod, because she couldn't curtsy in this position, the musicians resumed, as if they'd been waiting for a signal. Phineas started. They danced three sets and then he turned them as one, to start all over again. He knew the steps by heart, so he concentrated on her. Marina was so light and easy to lead on the dancefloor. Her skirts *swished* as they moved in a circular fashion, his gaze only on her. He could catch the scent of lilacs on her, an interesting one to detect in a room filled with hollies and evergreens for the season. It took every amount of energy he had to keep his hand at her waist and not at the small of her back, bringing her closer. But he could see the swell of her breasts rising rapidly and he wanted to believe that was because she was thrilled he'd pulled her out to dance with, and not fear.

Then he heard her stifled moan at the same moment her body relaxed. She was pleased, he determined, and spun her around the floor again, noticing her grin, though slight, at her lips.

As the music slowed to an ending, they stopped. He held her for just one minute more before he stepped back and bowed.

"My lady, what a pleasure it is to dance with you."

He swore he saw her blush. The room lit with light claps and the words of how they looked heavenly together filtered to his ears. Taking her hand, he walked her back to her cousin, and bowed. But when he looked into her gorgeous grey eyes, he saw fear and sadness flash across them. He schooled his features but was lost.

The woman who was sneaking inside his heart looked like she wanted nothing to do with him. That realization hit him hard. With a brief good evening, he spun on his heels and left.

Chapter Fourteen

MARINA, DRESSED IN HER NIGHTRAIL and wrapper, her arms wrapped around her, stood near the window in her bedroom. He had made a scene with her, allowing her to escape into a wild fantasy that he wanted her, only for it to end with him returning her to the party and then virtually running out of the ballroom. She closed her eyes tightly, determined not to cry, but inside, she shook, as if her whole world had collapsed.

But with her eyes closed, her memories of the dance flooded her thoughts. He held her so tight, almost demanding without any pain or fear. His eyes had turned dark blue, like they did in the cottage when he taught her how beautiful intimacy could be. And his jaw was set, like he was fighting to keep from scooping her away, to revisit that togetherness. She sighed. Perhaps those thoughts and the way her body yearned for his touch had made her believe that's what he wanted too…

"It's all packed, Lady Marina," the maid said.

Over her shoulder, she replied, "Thank you, Dottie. Good night."

"Good 'night, my lady."

When the door closed, Marina relaxed. She had left the ball not long after Phineas had, claiming she had a headache forming when the reality was she wanted to cry. It was all too much. The note from her father demanding her return for a quick marriage to Lord Goodsow. *Grrrr! He is Lord Goodwood!* She shook her head. It didn't matter, in the long run. The Marquis of Rockford didn't want her, and the rest of the lords here spent their time drooling over the other ladies, including her good cousin, and not her. *Oh, that was rubbish!* Self-pity was loathsome, and she was above that.

All this self-arguing made her angry and that, in turn, made her hot so she turned the latch on the French windows and took a step outside, onto the balcony. A rush of cold air hit her and for a moment, she relished it. It deadened the pain for a second and that was worth the freezing winds. Her toes curled.

"My, I believe it's a bit cold for a barefoot outing, though, I will tell you, your toes are lovely."

Shocked anyone was out, she tucked her toes under the wrapper and hugged herself tightly.

"Lord Rockford?"

"Considering our time together at the cottage, I would have thought that, as least here, in private, you would call me Phineas." He took a step closer, so the moonlight captured his figure. He was in his shirtsleeves and trousers with his shoes still on, she noted. In his hand was a whiskey glass.

She steeled herself. "I'm surprised to find you here, my lord." She on purpose left his true name out. How dare he abandon her at the ball then act like a jackanapes here...

His gaze locked onto hers. "I came to dance with you."

She frowned. Eyeing the glass in his hand, she

considered he might be drunk. "I'm hardly dressed to return below, my lord. And there are no musicians here on the balcony…"

It was then she heard the faint sound of the violins from below. He gave her a lazy smile.

"You were saying?" He stepped closer.

She could see the grin tugging at his lips, the loose lock of hair that fell over his brow and the relaxed look. He put the glass down and extended his hand.

"I'd be honored to have this dance with you."

Her heart skipped a beat. She was in her nightrail, for heaven's sake! But inside her, a voice screamed for her to dance with him.

"You danced with me at the ball but ran after you escorted me to my cousin, leaving me to believe you didn't enjoy my company," she argued. She fought hard to keep from shivering as the cold was seeping through the wrapper.

"That, dear lady, was never the case. I was pulled away by unforeseen circumstances."

She bit the inside of her lip, biting back the words she wanted to say. Instead she added, "It's freezing out here."

"I'll keep you warm," he replied, his tone low, slow and seductive.

This was madness, she decided, but that didn't keep her from putting her hand in his, throwing all caution and reason aside. The reality that she'd be married to a buffoon so she'd take the marquis up on his offer and soak in all of this decadence, banking the memory away for the days she was lonely at the old lord's home.

He spun her slowly to her right, gently leading

her to the tune that wafted up from below. She worried at first that he'd step on her toes but the memory of him dancing with Lady Forrest popped into her head, and the graceful moves he made. Within seconds, her fear evaporated. The faint hint of a smile tugged at his lips. Her hand rested on a sturdy and corded shoulder with the other held in a firm yet gentle grip. He was a master at this dance and he guided her around the balcony, taking all the cold out of the air. The fact was, being in his arms set up a burn deep inside her, that was stirred by the tingles of his touch and how that sensation raced through her. Her heart fluttered then started to beat wildly. She looked into his darkened blue gaze and tried to swallow the knot in her throat, but she couldn't.

Truth was, everywhere he touched her now lit her insides on fire. Her mouth went dry and she licked her bottom lip, pulling it inward. She wanted him to kiss her.

But the music faded and so did the dance steps. They stood, still poised to dance but not moving. Even as the chords below started again, they didn't move. She waited, unsure, knowing she should back away if he didn't, but she simply could not. Her gaze was locked on his, the intensity of his stare had her mesmerized, her heart beat loudly and the hunger started. She needed to feel his touch, and as much as she knew she shouldn't, the need wouldn't die.

Phineas held her hand probably tighter than was

needed and the one on her waist cinched a touch tighter, both happening before his thoughts caught up to him. Those grey eyes sparkled, her lips turned ruby, especially since her tongue licked the lower one, a move that caused his cock to harden. The rush of blood to his lower stomach, pooling in his groin surprised him, though he knew it shouldn't. Because this lady stirred a passion inside him he wasn't prepared for.

He wanted to taste her again and knew he shouldn't. It would lead to a road of no return. He was not to touch her. She was innocent, a lady for heaven's sake! Yet what if she wanted him to kiss her?

In the long run, it didn't matter. He leaned forward and locked his lips onto hers, pulling her fully into his embrace, his tongue tracing the line of hers in hopes she'd let him in. A tremor raced down her back and he knew he was right. When her lips parted, he wanted to shout to the heavens. In a split second, he kissed her deeply, exploring her and drinking in her taste. It was a blend of cherries, wine and her. He simply could not get enough and devoured her, with a thrill that she seemed equally exploratory, though her efforts were stilted, signs of a naïve experience.

When he pulled back, something he hadn't wanted to do but he realized he was crushing her. She was panting, a confused but round-eye look that told him she was curious. It sent another shiver through him and awakened the sleeping lion within his soul. She was curious but trembled, reminding him how cold it was. He scooped her up in his arms, where he kissed her hard as he walked down the balcony, three rooms down to the end. He pushed the French window open and took her into his bedchamber.

Once inside, he put her down, still exploring her mouth. She slid out of his arms, the mere touch of her clothed body next to his, the taste of her mouth and all the wonders of her body right at his touch nearly sent him over the edge. His hunger grew, intense and cautious. She was a lady, and untried, yet when her hands began to wander over his neck as they moved slowly, it drove him to growl into her mouth. He wanted more and moved his kisses to her jawline and then to her earlobe, where he tugged the skin that had earlier born an earring. She tipped back her head, opening new territory for him to explore and explore he did, his tongue delved down to her shoulders and open neckline. Her skin held that scent of lilacs, just like her hair had and it nearly drove him to the brink of insanity, as desire uncoiled within him, the need to be with her driving him.

But he stopped. A rational voice in the back of his head somehow managed to break through the lustful beast and told him to slow down. His course of action may not be wanted, and he'd better pay heed to what he was doing. He didn't think after Hester and her betrayal, that he'd want intimacy to any depth past superficial. Lord, even that sounded bad to him.

Finding himself confused, he held her close, grappling with his own desires and wondered how this woman had managed to dig past all his defenses. He stared into those gray eyes that now sparkled with hints of blue. Her lips were swollen from his kisses, but she didn't move. Breathing heavily, he found she matched his cadence and noted how her nipples had hardened, their pearled tips were on display, no doubt the result of his touch. Damn!

Marina was lost in an emotional sea of confusion and desire, hot and cold. They shouldn't be here, in his room, with her in her night rail. But his chest and stomach hardened by muscles she had no idea gentlemen might have. Heavens knows Lord Goodsow had nothing hard about his middle! She shook that thought, but it lingered.

She swore a part of her screamed at her for letting Phineas get this close, but a larger tone urged her to want more. She swallowed the lump in her throat, feeling the tingle he'd ignited which still sent fiery shots through her. Phineas was like a Greek god, his kisses divine and it didn't take much thought for her to realize the bulge that nudged into her as he brought her closer was his cock, hard for her. *Dear Lord!* Merely considering that made her hot and flustered. It made her body weep in anticipation of his company. No lady should think that!

A vision of her and this future groom, imitating what she just had, made her go cold. If she had held the memories of dancing with him outside for future frigid nights as a wife, she realized if she let the marquis continue, she could lose her maidenhead to him. As a man who showed her true passion, he could be the memory that would save her in the years to come.

As that idea took hold in her head, she knew it also affected her heart, for she realized, at this moment, she was doomed. She wanted more. She might never get the chance, but she did have the chance to decide whom to give her maidenhead to, and now, it seemed that her soul craved it be the lord before her. As he took a step back and opened his mouth with what she feared was good-bye, she stumbled.

"Phineas, please," she begged, the words spilling from her mouth before she could think straight. Her heart thudded wildly. But the risk to be so bold to be with one who would give her the memory to recall in an otherwise dull future just had to be taken. She held her breath, waiting for his reply.

Phineas could not believe what he heard. His blood raced so fast, it pounded in his ears and he feared he might have misunderstood. He worked hard to decipher what was happening and failed on every mark. His inner beast had pulled her up into his arms and he brought her to his room – *his room*. He didn't want her cousin to suddenly appear. He strained to hear any sound from the party below and luckily, he heard the cello, so Lady Ruth should be there.

His chamber, though, wasn't any more ideal place and it clearly indicated that he wanted her. She should run. She should do a great many things but asking him to continue was not what he expected. He eyed her carefully. There was an aura around her, one that made his body decide his reply to her—he pulled her back into his embrace and kissed her deeply. She molded her body against his, returning his kiss just as deeply.

He growled, and everything happened like a crazy whirlwind. Access to her mouth encouraged him to go further. It took seconds to pull the ties on her wrapper and he shoved it off her shoulders, letting it fall in a heap to the floor. Attired in only the nightrail, she shuddered under his touch and he'd wager she'd never been so exposed to a man before, but he'd push her past that in just moments.

Marina unclasped her hands and her fingertips traced over his shoulders, rubbing down his chest with her palms. Every inch she touched, despite the waistcoat and shirt, burned his skin, and he wanted to ask for more. She traced up to his neck and slowly, in a seductive melody, found his collar and the neckcloth beneath. He felt her fingers tug at the knot, freeing the ends and she yanked the piece of cloth off, tossing it to the floor, while she returned to his collar and began to undue the buttons. With the placard loose, she worked on his waistcoat. He burned, trying hard to be patient when he truly wanted to rip all of it off by himself, basically to save the time, though her ministrations he couldn't tear from, so he worked on the ties for the nightrail. It took less time to pull those, he thought, than her on his but they both tugged at the same time. They should've laughed at that, but he witnessed how dark her gray eyes turned and he knew the battle she fought and lost.

He stepped back and tore his clothes away, leaving him bare-chested and in his stocking feet. With a curved lopsided grin, he took the fabric at her shoulders and pulled upward. She stood still, allowing him to gather the nightrail up. It was like opening a present wrapped in gold as he held his breath. Pulling, he gathered the material and yanked it off, tossing it to the side like paper so he could see what he'd opened.

Marina stood before him, nothing on. She was perfection. Her breasts were full but not too big, her waist narrowed, like an hourglass with beautifully rounded hips. Ivory-skinned perfection with rosy pearl-tipped breasts and silky dark curls at the apex of her thighs, she was like Aphrodite and it took every effort not to devour her.

"You are beautiful," he murmured and before she could say a word, he took her in his arms and kissed her again. The warmth of her skin, the silky smoothness made her delectable and his cock throbbed painfully. He had to have her. He bent and picked her up to gently lay her on the bed with all intentions of quickly striping his trousers off and climbing in but before he could move, she reached for the trail of buttons on the trousers and began to undo them. As the flap freed and his straining member sprang forward, he couldn't move. When she finished and glanced up at him, all sense of rationality fled.

Rarely did Marina ever bare herself and now, she couldn't help the goose bumps that formed. A slight chill raced up her spine and she felt her nipples harden, the tight nubs tingling for attention. Her toes curled under again.

While she stood naked, he was half way there, bare-chested and muscular, she wanted to touch, to feel the flex of those muscles. She had no idea they could be so well defined. But if her gaze lowered, she saw the bulge in his trousers. His erection had pushed against her when she was dressed. Now, she had no barriers and he was straining to be free of his. So she'd help and reached for the buttons.

The heel of her hand had brushed next to the hardness as she located the buttons. He nearly jumped when she nudged it and couldn't stop the smile that formed to turn the tables. He stood frozen to the spot while she did her magic, releasing them all, and the trousers dropped to the floor like her wrapper had. She licked her lips, which caused him to moan. Puzzled, she frowned, and his response was to take her mouth with his as he lowered to the bed.

Complete naked, they kissed hard, halfway rolling to the edge of the bed. He kissed down her neck and she couldn't keep the mewl from leaking out. As his fingers darted swiftly down her chest, he found one of her breasts and cupped the mound of flesh, his thumb pad gliding over the erect nipple and the minor touch made her back arch with excitement rolling through her. When his tongue raced down her chest and the top of the creamy mound, he took her nipple into his mouth, teasing it with his tongue and scraping it with his teeth.

"Oh, Phineas! Oh!" She raised her breasts to meet his onslaught.

He suckled her right breast, teasing the nub with his teeth and tongue as she moaned. Then, he ran to the left one, his tongue blazing a trail across her breastbone. She wiggled, trying to get closer but he seemed to know just how to stay a smidgen away, to taunt her more, she was sure. Determined to touch him, she put her hand on his chest, using the other to keep her stable, looking to find his own core when he tugged at the nipple. As it pearled hard, tingles raced up, into her chest and then roared to her abdomen, where she could tell she was wet and swelling.

She had to adjust her legs, propping one up, giving her space and that's when she felt a cool breeze skate across the lips to her core. She shivered, melting to his touch. Instantly, she went to stabilize her rocking body and put her palm on his nude hip, kneeling it as she inched closer to his cock.

"Uh, uh, uh," he mumbled against her stomach. "Just a minute."

Before she could even breath again, he nudged her hips down and her legs sprawled enough that he could bend and kiss her nether lips, his tongue darting out across the slit. Marina nearly exploded off the bed. He licked again, and she knew there was no escape. She wanted what he was doing. So when he flattened her hips to the bed and threw one of her legs over his lowered shoulder, she was speechless. Her body shook when he licked gently up her inner thigh to her core and he settled there, holding her hands with one hand and adjusting her body to give him access to below.

"Phineas, please!" She begged him, but she wasn't sure what she was begging for. His wet caress of her nether lips set off a fire that burned brighter.

It didn't matter what she did, his tongue slipped inside her slit and fireworks exploded in her head, especially as he moved up and found a nub there that was so sensitive, she was sure she'd burst into flames. When he took that nub in his lips and sucked there, the well within her womanhood exploded and her body wept. One of his hands was on her thigh before she realized that he was going to take a finger and insert it inside her. The sensation blew her thoughts around. His digit slid right in and she bit back the small burn that happened when he put that finger fully inside her. Slowly, he withdrew that appendage right as she started to enjoy the sensation.

"Oh, no, please don't stop!"

"You're very wet," he whispered, kissing her neck.

She opened her mouth to tell him it was his fault except his hips moved and she could tell his cock was at her thigh, the silken hot flesh was heavy with desire. Curious, she reached down and found the member, stiff and hard. Her hand wrapped around it, squeezing slightly. He moaned.

"Be careful," he spit out.

With a careful caress, she slid her hand up and down his erection, feeling it pulse in her grip. Pleased, she took a better hold to do better but she never got the chance because he nipped her nub and inserted his finger again. Then added another. It was tight, but she could accommodate it. As she rocked to his touch, he moaned to hers. Her speed increased and suddenly, it all stopped. He grabbed her wrist.

He stared into her eyes. It was a frustrating moment because she was open, wet and wanting—everything decent ladies were not supposed to be. But another insertion and she nearly bucked off the bed. Her hand lost its grip on him and he moved, tipping her hips up slightly. His cock was there, the head of it wet and without his touch, her core wept. She adjusted, moving closer when he gave her a long look, his breath in pants and his eyes dark.

She nodded. She wanted him and the feel of him deep inside her. It was a wrong request, so she held back from making it. The tip of his erection butted against her nether lips and she moved closer still.

"Marina, are you sure?"

She nodded, the need to have him in her growing. She bit her tongue as his hands came to her hips, widening them a bit more. He bent and gave her another lick and she mewled, tilting her hips up and in that split second, when she moaned her satisfaction, his cock slid into her.

Sheer pain rippled through her. Quickly, she tilted her head to scream when he kissed her hard. Confused when he pulled back, she laid there, realizing he hadn't moved, so she grew accustomed to the intrusion Now, he moved, slightly withdrawing his member and then plunging back in. The pain subsided, and she kept on meeting his thrusts. The deeper he went, the more she felt her body widen, she wanted to scream until she grew used to it. Finally, he was in. she felt his bollocks slam into her as he entered her.

It didn't take long for their rhythm to increase. With each invasion, Marina's sheath turned to liquid and she tightened, to try to keep him from withdrawing, which made him growl and increase his speed. She matched him, feeling a pressure building. She was at a crux, a primitive need for more when the next thrust hit hard. His cock fully buried in her, touching her womb and she exploded, a million stars filling her vision as her body gripped his member hard.

The pressure increased. He entered her fully, her core taking him fully and it tightened around him. He knew he was close to climax, but he worked hard to keep from it until she shattered beneath him. But as they went faster, he lost control. A final thrust, one that dated back to the beginning of time, made him drive right into her and the moment he hit her womb, he came, filling her with his seed. As he drained into her, an intense joy filled him. Despite all his denials to never fall for love or marriage, this woman had found her way into his heart. He smiled as he finished and withdrew, falling next to her on the bed.

He kissed her shoulder and whispered, "I love you."

Pulling the cover up over them, he took her into his arms and fell deep asleep, a happiness he never thought he'd have blanketing them both. Until tomorrow, his last thought said, contended his future wife was in his arms.

Chapter Fifteen

MARINA STOOD ABSOLUTELY STILL AS the modiste circled her, pins and twill tape in hand. The woman chatted continuously about how gorgeous the dress would be and how the guests would gush compliments. But she didn't care. It was just a contractual marriage, a few words spoken that would bind her to an old man till one of them died. She was utterly convinced that would be her.

Her mind drifted back to Rockford Hall and the lord, who had swept her off her feet—quite literally. It had only been two days, but she'd remembered that night in her head as if she was at the theater and the play was repeated over and over again.

After Phineas had taken her to the exquisite heights, when the stars exploded in a fantastic array of colors and her body shattered, as she cooled down and realized he was still inside her, she reveled in that moment. His cock throbbed inside her core and it was a feeling she never wanted to lose. He had kissed her and pulled her close after his member faded and she swore he claimed he loved her. It was a cherished thrill, and she clung to that moment, afraid it'd disappear as time moved forward. As they snuggled on his bed, she could feel his breath on her shoulder become more steady and slower. She moved a tad to test if he was asleep and he didn't stir. Taking a deep breath, she carefully slipped out of his arms, praying he'd wake and stop her, but he didn't. Once out of bed, she glanced at him. He was halfway curled on the mattress, the bed sheet covered up to his hips, hiding his cock. She halted her escape to drink in this memory because she had to leave. Not only get out of his room, but out of his house.

She had been surprised how easy it was for her to leave the party. Aunt Clare had had enough and longed to return to a quieter lifestyle. As Marina threw her belongings into the travel trunk, her aging aunt spoke with Lady Margaret to watch Ruth, for there was no point dragging her away if the other lady would take her under her wing. A quick note to call the carriage and away they went, back to London and her father's house.

Lord Lockhart had been thrilled she'd returned so promptly. He had discussed matters with the rector, been assured Goodwood was obtaining a special license so they could be married before the Christmas sermons. All she needed was her dress and, from the sight of the overly gaudy ensemble with all its lace and pearled tulle, her future husband was footing the bill. She wasn't sure if she should laugh or cry over the whole thing. So, instead, she stood still and in that moment of quiet, she heard him.

"I love you."

Phineas' voice echoed in her head. She shut her eyes, hoping it was true, and praying it wasn't…. Despite all her work to forget the mere whisper of those words had destroyed her. Her eyes filled with tears and she forced the lump in her throat to go down. Crying would not change anything. The marquis did not want a wife, though she did not know why, and she was bound to marry without any other suitor fighting for her hand.

One thing she was sure of and that was she'd never regret giving him her virginity. The moment she saw her intended husband, she clenched her fists not to run. Goodwood was jovial in front of her father, but alone with him he made her want to wretch. He spoke little, mostly complimented her and how he was such a lucky man. It took every effort she had not to run.

"My, don't you look lovely," Aunt Clare said. "How are we feeling?"

"Thank you." She managed to smile. "I feel good."

Her aunt waggled her lips, raising a brow. "You looked lost, or perhaps sad."

Was she that obvious? She bit her inner cheek and forced a laugh. "I think its exhaustion from the party and the whirlwind of fittings and planning for the wedding."

"That is true, my dear, but your father wants your wedding to be a magnificent celebration. That does require proper planning, more so when it happens so quickly." She motioned for her to spin. "Truly lovely. That champagne color looks grand on you."

"Yes, I believe it does."

Marina glanced up and found her father standing there, a grin on his lips. The earl looked at her up and down. She felt like she was a cow at market.

"Won't you say thank you?" He gave her a sideways look, the type she'd seen all her life, when he knew the answer he wanted she didn't.

"Father, I request to postpone this marriage—"

"Whatever for?" he demanded. She saw the pink tone that came to his chubby cheeks when his anger stirred.

"I simply wish to enjoy the holidays—"

"Which you shall," he interrupted. "As a newly-wed bride."

Her insides tightened. Anger fought to take hold, but she kept her mask of civility on. "I wish to have a season."

"Preposterous!"

"Why, papa?" Her vision started to blur but she'd not back down. She might not have her marquis, but …

"The ton's Season is nothing better than a farmer's market of sorts, of parading ladies like they are breeding stock to a bunch of titles no one cares for!"

She blinked. "That is not true. You yourself have frequented them. That is where you met mama."

"A fine lady indeed, but long gone from this world." He breathed deep. "This is a good match."

"He's old enough to be you!" She blurted the truth and instantly covered her mouth with her hands.

"Marina."

She'd seen that look on his face for her entire life. The look of he was in charge and his decision would stand. But this was her life, and to cut it short…

Every fiber in her body screamed to say Phineas' name so it took every ounce she had to try to stop this another way. "Why? Why would you condemn me to marry an old man?"

Lockhart shooed Clare out of the room and closed the door to the parlor. "You will not talk like that to your father! Lord Goodwood is an honorable man and respected. Hopefully he will be able to curb your behavior that is showing at this point." He swallowed. "Children or none is not part of the bargain."

"Bargain?" Her heart sunk. "My marriage is a bargain?"

Lockhart's hands shuffled, like they did when he was caught in a fib—or worse. "Times are hard, at the moment. His ability to save our home is worthy a marriage as payment."

Her eyes widened as the sick feeling swirled in her stomach. "No, you can't."

"But I can. And I will. The Lockhart reputation will be saved. Now," he grabbed her shoulders and bent to kiss her cheek. "Be a good girl and look good for your wedding."

When the door latched closed behind him, Marina's legs buckled, and she became a heap on the floor. Marry the sow to save her father's reputation. She was afraid to blink, to move even. Finally, the memories of her night, giving herself to the marquis, made sense. She'd use them to get her through this.

"I love you," Phineas repeated, and she prayed to God, he did because right now, she felt more abandoned and sacrificed than loved.

The tears started.

Two Days Earlier....

THE MARQUIS OF ROCKFORD STRETCHED. For the first time in a long time, he had slept. Truly slept. The sun lit the room, despite the curtains being drawn and as he savored the moment, the light brought back last night and his lady. He turned, expecting her there and found he was the only one in the bed. He frowned. She should have been there unless she had slipped back to her room. He lay back on his pillow, slightly more relaxed. That was the only conclusion that worked, and it made sense. The scandal would fly through this group, he speculated. Not that he didn't have that attached to his name anyway, thanks to Hester.

On that note, he scowled and leapt off the mattress. He called for Hinds, who arrived with lightning speed. The butler said nothing, and Phineas hoped it stayed that way. He would divert any conversation away from the double indention on the bed and the disarrayed bedclothes. The lilac scent, though, might be harder to dismiss, unless he was the only one who could still sniff that in the air.

"Sir, they await you in the dining room," Hinds told him as he helped cinch the last button on the waistcoat.

Phineas headed down the stairs, his mood more improved than it had been throughout the entire holiday festivities. In fact, he discovered he was nearly skipping toward the dining room and that made him halt to recompose himself.

Walking into the room, he found his sister, Featherton, Marina's cousin Ruth, along with a handful of others. But no Marina. His heart skidded for a second, but he schooled his features with a practiced ease that now grated on his nerves. A sudden desire to not be the lord of the estate hit him and the pressure that came with that, like wedding and bedding for an heir to continue the line. Expect now, he may have found the woman worthy to become his marchioness.

"Good morning, brother. You're up rather late this day," Anne stated before she took a sip of her tea.

Featherton quickly took a sip of his own, though Phineas still heard a murmur of a smirk.

He shot them a look as he took his seat. "Good morning, Anne." He took his own cup, which the footman had just filled, and drank, swallowing a caustic remark he wanted to make. He'd have to check with Lady Margaret, to make sure his darling sister had not had her own romantic night with Featherton, for they looked a little too pleased to suit him.

"It has been a lovely house party, my lord." Ruth gave him a genuine smile.

The rest of the table also chimed in. Anne watched him carefully, and that pose made Phineas wonder what was in that head of hers.

"Lady Anne, as always, is a gracious hostess," Featherton remarked, raising his cup to her.

Phineas glared at his friend. While the compliment was valid, for Anne was always the better hostess, coming from his friend it set off a nerve that burned. If Featherton and Anne had come close to what he exchanged with Marina last night, there would be pistols at dawn!

Anne bowed her head in acknowledgement of the praise. "It was the company here that made it so enjoyable. Thank you all for coming."

Phineas sat, downing his breakfast without much being said, listening to the group relate more about last night. Patiently, he waited for Marina and prayed she'd arrive soon but by the end, she was nowhere to be seen. He felt bereft without her and that was a new emotion, one he wasn't sure he wanted to acknowledge.

As the guests finished and got up to leave, many headed toward the front. Outside the front windows, carriages awaited, their horses stomping in the snow, eager to get moving. Phineas followed the crowd, still waiting for his future bride to be fleeing down the stairs as Ruth went to the doorway, cloak on.

Anne hugged each of the ladies, promising to see them soon in London. Featherton stood near her, mostly speaking to the men, who too, donned their cloaks. Phineas watched them all pour out the front door and leave. With the numbers dwindling, he began to worry. Where was she?

Only a few were left when he started to pace. Something must be wrong, he decided. She was sick or still asleep, a plausible cause considering he'd kept her up late, introducing her to the world of intimacy. He forced himself to relax. Entering his library, he went to his desk and sat down.

"Phineas, what is wrong?"

He turned and found Anne at his library door. "Nothing, my dear. Why would you ask?"

She tilted her head. "You do not seem to be

yourself this morning."

"All is well."

"Excellent." She spun on her heels to leave.

"Anne, wait," he called her back. "Has Lady Marina taken ill? I did not see her this morning, to wish her safe travel."

Anne's eyes narrowed, and she rolled back on her heels. "Really? I thought you of all people would know. She's gone."

His heart stopped. "Pardon me? Before breakfast?"

"Yes. It did seem a bit odd. She apparently had a missive to return home promptly."

He stood, his quick response knocking the chair back, scraping the floor. "She left early for a note? Is her father well?"

Anne laughed. "No. Apparently, she's to marry."

Phineas blinked, stunned. *"Marry?"*

Chapter Sixteen

IT WAS A BEAUTIFUL DAY. The sun shone brightly, the birds chirped, though it remained cold with a layer of white snow blanketing the area. The streets were compacted so travel was normal, though few ladies ventured out. It was the holidays and time for close gatherings of friends and family. If it wasn't for the Rockford party merely three days ago, Marina knew at this moment, she'd have missed the warmth of the holiday for right now, at Covington Church, the blood in her veins was as icy as the roads were outside.

Everything was moving too fast. She wanted to remain in her sweet memories of curling up with Phineas and the ecstasy he'd brought her to that night. But her father was determined to bind her to this aged, overweight but wealthy old man. That special license, the holidays streaming closer and a rector who claimed it was now or not till well after Epiphany. Therefore, the seamstress had slaved all night to complete the dress that no one of note would see for a stream of vows that made her his. She shivered.

The door opened, and Ruth slipped inside. "Marina! When I heard, I hurried over. So this is why you fled from the party. I thought it was something the marquis said." She stopped, and her eyes opened wide. "You look beautiful!"

She laughed nervously. *Something the marquis said...* "I did not *run* from there except for the note you remember I received."

"I didn't recall it saying you had to leave immediately."

"Perhaps I did not share that with you." Heavens, she had run, and it was due to something he'd said. *I love you.* Better him than the man who weighed five times what he weighed. He'll crush her! Might go better than dying out of sheer boredom....

Ruth walked over to the lilies that decorated the room. "These have no scent to speak of. Pity." She turned to Marina again. "I had had hopes the marquis might whisk you away to become his marchioness."

Marina, who had taken a sip from her teacup, sputtered. "Why would you think that?"

"Well, the way he danced with you. He appeared very, very close, if you don't mind me saying so." She smelled another bouquet and grimaced. "What did he tell you? Because he appeared to say something."

Marina swallowed the lump in her throat. "Say something to me? Nothing I can recall. As to the dance, it was the waltz, if you'll recall. He meant nothing by it, I am sure."

"Mmmmmm."

Marina waited but nothing more was said. She had left Ruth behind to enjoy the end of the party, or so she told Aunt Clare, but reality was, she couldn't handle her patience if the girl was brought with them, for she'd be asking why and what could she say? So she retreated to her father's note and this exchange.

"If all Goodsow wanted was a quick nuptials, why the dress?" Ruth continued, obviously changing subjects as if the party they'd attended all week was nothing. "It is beautiful but rather fancy for a quick exchange, is it not?"

"It was part of my trousseau he gave me as a wedding present." She sighed. Ruth was correct. This was not a wedding for the gossip rags to write about. All that would be mentioned, if at all, was that Lord Goodwood had married… "And as he is to be my husband, please refrain from using Goodsow."

Ruth stopped, a questioning look flashed across her face. "Truly? Or are you afraid I'll call you Lady Goodsow?" She winked. It made Marina laugh.

"Yes, my lady," she bowed. "I'll do my utmost."

"Thank you."

"But really, I thought the Marquis of Rockford would have been here to prevent this tragedy."

Marina, who had moved to put her teacup on the sideboard, stopped, her ears ringing. "Why ever would you say that?"

She could see her cousin's lips curve upright though she tried to look occupied staring at the chapel's registry. "Oh, I'm not sure. Perhaps it was the way he lingered over breakfast on the morning we left. His gaze constantly looking at the door, as if he expected you there."

"Oh, posh, that is nothing." Or was it?

Ruth's brows rose. "And his happy attitude, much more obvious than any other time, faded when you failed to appear. In fact, he looked downright sullen."

"Ruth, truly...."

"Well, it was clear to the rest of us he was in love with you."

There was that word again. She snorted at the thought.

Now Ruth looked shocked. "You did not think we noticed the night in the wood during the snowstorm, did you?"

"I spent it at the gardener's cottage, just like he said."

"Marina, you fell off a horse and managed to crawl to a cottage out there, and spend the night in the cold? When did you learn to start a fire?" She stepped closer. "And where was he that night? The stable lad, Kenny, claimed he saw you two ride in just before dawn. Not a normal hour for a marquis."

Marina cheeks turned warm. "Nothing happened..."

"So you did spend a night with him!"

*More than one...*She withheld that second one from her. "He saved me from that fall. I hit my head on a tree stump and he saved me from succumbing to the cold. That's all that happened." And that was the truth.

Ruth frowned. "He ruined you that night by being out with you. You know that. Why didn't he marry you?"

"He said he won't marry at this time," Marina answered glumly. "Said he is still mourning his betrothed."

"Posh! He is not! Lord Riverbend told me the story. She died from complications..."

Marina frowned. "Complications?"

"Yes!" Ruth leaned forward. "She was enceinte."

"No wonder he still mourns her."

"It wasn't his child!"

Marina's heart skipped a beat. "I beg your pardon?"

"Lady Hester apparently did not wish to wait and took knowledge of the flesh before her engagement. But being a good family, she wasn't tossed, as if she was a hog bone. No. Her marriage would save her from being called slattern and the child a bastard."

"And the marquis knew of her impurity?"

"According to Lord Riverbend, the marquis did not, until the wedding banns had been called and she turned ill."

"Oh, my," Marina murmured, her mind whirling at such a thought.

"And there's more." Ruth relished in storytelling and gossip. It shouldn't surprise Marina at all the girl had searched for more. "Her death might have been caused by her."

Marina couldn't hear, her heart pounded so hard. No wonder he hadn't looked for another bride. His first betrayed him. "Now I see why he was so cool toward us."

"Cool? Maybe to everyone else but not you."

The room turned warm and the dress too confining, making her want to squirm. She refused to give the memories that much credit. In an attempt to get the subject off the marquis and a long-term attraction she doubted he had, Marina thought it best to change the topic. "Appears you and Lord Riverbend have been keeping company, so to speak."

Ruth smiled broadly. "He is talking to Papa, asking for permission to court me."

Pleasantly shocked, though she should have seen this coming, Marina smiled. "That is wonderful!"

Her cousin was beaming. She was so lucky, Marina thought. Perhaps she could visit her often and take a break from being under the old man's control.

"Oh, Marina, don't cry!"

Marina blinked hard, totally unaware the tears had formed. She had cried too much lately. "I'll be fine. Really. Lord Goodwood is not that horrible. He's actually been quite sweet."

"But he's too old for you!"

She shook her head. "You are well aware of others who marry men beyond their years."

"Posh! They also have lovers!"

"Like who?" she asked softly.

Her cousin bit her lip. "Give me a moment. I'll think of one."

Marina snorted. A lover. It was an intriguing thought but not likely. She wouldn't put it past her husband, but ladies rarely ventured that risk. And she was speaking the truth. Goodwood had greeted her warmly on her return, promised to answer all her desires, keep her a wealthy lady. He purchased her trousseau, paid for all the ceremony and he did have a warm smile. She would do her duty and grin all the way, even if it was forced.

"Marina, don't give up hope. What if the Marquis of Rockford came calling for your hand?" Ruth looked so hopeful, probably because of her good fortune.

"Ruth," she took her cousin's hands in hers and

gave her cheek a kiss. "If Lord Rockford was that distraught, as you say, that was well over three days ago. More than sufficient time to race here and save me. He's very handsome, of good station and has the fortune to take any lady as wife. It's good. I will be fine. His lordship has promised me it will be good, and my father's misfortune solved. Please, give me your good wishes. Please," she begged.

Ruth's lips thinned but she finally nodded. "I always want the best for you."

Marina squeezed her hands. She would be fine… but the hint of the marquis lingered. It would take a lifetime to forget him.

It took Phineas half the day, arguing with himself, as to what to do next. The sting of Hester was still raw. He never thought she would have betrayed him considering their union was a practical one for their families and she'd never given him a hint that she was against it. So when the truth was revealed, he'd retreated to the countryside, after days of her funeral where he pasted a mourning face on, took condolences for his loss, since most of the ton named him the father of the child she carried, followed by a three-day drinking binge and withdrawal to the country estate, where the wall he could build around himself took hold with a vow not to marry.

The Christmas house party was Anne's request. He'd long figured it was her ruse to get Featherton there, but as the party dwindled and the guests left, he began to view it differently. It may have been the first objective, but it apparently served as a means to get him back into society. *Touché*, he thought, but what the cost. Another lady who abandoned him for another, until he heard of her future husband. Goodwood was old enough to be her grandfather and was portly enough to barely fit through a carriage door, let alone consider a horseback ride!

The more he thought about it, the lingering memory of when he took her, finally battered at the wall he'd so carefully built. He remembered telling her, during the aftermath of their lovemaking, that he loved her. It didn't matter to him at the time she hadn't replied but now, he needed to know. It was an odd quirk, but an inner voice told him to race to London and save her from a marriage she wouldn't survive, or so he believed.

He took off toward London, to find Lady Marina, only to discover he was too late. No one was at her townhouse in the city. The butler looked rather terse that Phineas had banged on the door and inquired about his mistress, so his answer was polite but short, that she was getting married. And the man had the audacity to close the door on him! He stood here, shocked, but why should the servant offer more? After all, Phineas arrived, jumped off the saddle and ran up the stairs, his own deportment rather shabby, he was sure. No lord would arrive in such a manner, spewing questions without stating who he was, nor did he come in the manner of a proper lord.

He inhaled deeply and turned to get back on his horse to leave when a carriage pulled up and the driver pulled the door open as a maid climbed out and walked to the door. When the door opened, he halfway considered following the girl, only she didn't enter. Another came out, dressed in finery for a wedding. It was Lady Ruth. Phineas sprang at the opportunity and opened the opposite carriage door to sneak in.

Ruth pulled her dress train in and sat, arranging her skirts before the carriage started and settled her skirts without glancing up. Phineas sat still, waiting. When she finally glanced forward, she found Phineas there.

"Och! My Lord! You scared me!"

"Apologies. I did not mean to startle you." He paused. "I need to know. Did your cousin marry?"

She shook her head. "That is where I'm headed now."

"Damn!" He slumped back on the seat, drained from racing to stop a terrible mistake. The sound of the carriage wheels turning and the horse's hooves driving into him, like nails in his coffin. The silence was deadening.

Ruth gave him an odd look. "You came to London, to see Marina?"

He wanted to shoot a sarcastic answer but that's when he noticed her smiling. "Yes."

"Lord Rockford, you appear like a fallen sparrow," she started. "But all is not lost. Marina is in love with you. I know it."

He snorted. "But she's marrying another."

Ruth shrugged. "If you feel the same, which your presence here seems to indicate, surely you could present your case. That is, if you love her."

"I told her I did, when we—" He let his voice fade. He couldn't tell her cousin of their intimacy.

That was inappropriate, though if he won Marina's hand, he'd blurt it to the skies.

Ruth's grin widened. "I'd wondered." She laughed into her handkerchief, trying to hide her face. "I told her that you did."

His eyes widened. "When did you do that?"

She tried to give him an innocent look. "Earlier, before I came home to change for this." She leaned forward. "Please, dear Lord Rockford, save her from a life of dullness and no love. It is not a marriage she wants, but she is simply following her duty, or so she claims."

That he understood. He looked out the window absently. "Family. I understand."

"No!" she spat. "I see you look devastated. You must be in love, to have ridden here and appearing like that, to see her."

Phineas snorted and looked down. He looked like a peasant, having grabbed his coat and jumping on Star's back. His stockings had mud splatters from riding over roads where the snow was melting, and he no doubt reeked of horse. "Hardly the ensemble for courtship."

"Courtship? You must be more like a savior than a proper gentleman at this point."

"Then, Lady Ruth, take me to her."

Chapter Seventeen

PHINEAS RACED UP THE CHURCH stairs, his blood pounding. He could hear the organ chiming away and he prayed it was the beginning of the ceremony and not the end. Of course, the other fear was he was at the wrong chapel. He'd gone by what the Ruth told him, but he'd left her to, so he didn't make matters worse by being seen with her when it was Marina he came for. At the church doors, he slid inside and waited for his eyes to adjust from the bright sunshine outside to the dark antechamber to the church.

Before him, he saw a sparsely filled church, decorated in evergreens and the scent of them with the lemon polish filled his nose. It was a small wedding, with so few there, a stab of pity hit him. Marina needed a gallant wedding, not a quickly thrown together one. He found her at the altar, with Lord Goodwood. Heavens, her height matched his and all Phineas could think was how the short rotund man was the wrong match.

Marina looked beautiful. The champagne silk dress draped her body, the fabric falling like a waterfall to the floor. The pearl and lace trim accented her neckline and sleeves. Her hair was piled high in curls and pearls with ribbons intertwined. She looked like a delicate swan and her partner a clown. Phineas growled.

He must have muttered that too loudly. The entire chamber turned and stared.

"Lord Rockford?" he heard Marina faintly.

"My lord!" Goodwood added.

"Lord Rockford," the rector interjected. "If you'll have a seat, my lord."

"No."

He heard the handful of guests muttering softly.

"My lord?" The rector again.

Phineas stood, unable to move. He pleaded with her, begging her with his look to come to him. It was insanity, he was sure.

"My lord, do I understand you object to this union?"

"Yes, indeed I do." There, he'd said it. He started walking down the aisle.

"On what grounds?" A man from the bride's family side argued.

Phineas didn't look or answer. It was her father, he decided. He'd deal with him later.

"This is preposterous!" Goodwood protested.

Phineas ignored them all, focusing just on Marina. Her gaze questioned him, but she remained quiet.

"Lady Marina," he said, taking her hand and kneeling before them all, his attention focused solely on her. He could feel her hand tremble. "Will you marry me?"

Chaos broke all around them. Goodwood threw up his hands, complaining to the rector to stop this. The lord in the front row, her father he assumed, also roared, at Marina and the rector, to ignore him. The guests all talking, except for Ruth, who he saw out of the corner of his eye, smiling as she stood to the side of Marina as her bridesmaid.

Marina's gaze widened but instead of paling at being cornered, as it were, her cheeks blushed. That gave him hope. She hadn't answered yet. He prayed fervently that she'd say yes, but as the seconds climbed, anxiety snaked down his back. But he refused to move.

"Marry me," he implored again softly. His heart thudded hard. If she didn't, he knew he'd die.

Marina couldn't move. She was frozen. What she prayed for was right before her and it made her tremble, that it wasn't real but a cruel jest.

"I love you."

Her heart skipped a beat.

"Lady Marina, please," Goodwood pleaded.

She finally turned toward the rector, but the good man only waited. "Reverend, may I have a minute?"

"Yes, Lady Lockhart."

"How dare you let this man interrupt *my* wedding!" Goodwood complained again.

"He objected to the union, my lord. Now we will see why."

Goodwood grumbled. She saw her father fuming, but Ruth was grinning like a child who stole a cookie but was never caught. What had she done to encourage this?

Phineas remained kneeling. He'd asked her the question she'd hoped he would. But he had also told her he never would marry. Why now? Love? How did she know he wouldn't change his mind?

Finally, she said, "You told me you'd not marry. What has changed?"

He inhaled, but never broke his gaze, nor released her hand. "I was engaged before, but the lady betrayed me. She died trying to cover her mistake. It burned my heart, to think she'd do that before we wed, how would I know she wouldn't do so again? I did not love her, but we could've had a placid marriage, like the one I just interrupted."

She shuddered. He was right.

"And now?" She needed to know.

"I realized, after you left, that there was a hole in my heart, one that would never feel whole again without you. I fell in love with you that day of the hunt when you met Petunia. You did not run, like a frightened girl. And later," he paused. "I know why you did what you did."

A flash of embarrassment raced through her. That night that she gave herself to him. He now understood why she'd lain with him, now that he saw what her marriage would have been like. The flurry of voices around her, which she drowned out, knowing others were guessing the same.

"I love you, Marina. Please, marry me."

Her father shouted to deny him. Goodwood still argued loudly. But she knew if she denied his proposal, her heart would die in a loveless marriage. Her soul screamed what she hadn't said, that she loved him.

"Phineas," she started, her voice sounding strong. "I love you and yes, I will marry you."

Phineas smiled broadly. He was so handsome, she thought, squeezing his hand that held hers. Quickly, he stood, pulled her into his arms and crushed her lips with a deep-ending kiss. It was hard and fast, one where he devoured her as he held her tight.

The organ player quickly banged on the keyboard, the music light and the whole chamber rang with voices, but she heard nothing other than the sound of her heart, which now sang loudly.

He loved her, and she loved him. "Merry Christmas, Phineas," she whispered.

"Merry Christmas, my love," he replied and kissed her again.

On that day, during the holidays, the wedding turned to one no longer seeming grim and imprisoning. It was joyful and happy. They were one, with love blessing them forever.

The End

GET THIS BOOK FOR FREE!

Join me for more fun, learning about upcoming novels, cover reveals, being on the team to see new stories first and all else an author and her muse can share!

Click to find out more!
www.ginadanna.com

Other Books By Gina

THE LORDS & LADIES & LOVE SERIES
To Catch a Lady, Book 1
To Dance with a Lord, Book 2
To Kiss a Lady, Book 3

THE GLADIATORS SERIES
Love & Vengeance, Book I
Love & Lies, Book II
Great & Unfortunate Desires
This Love of Mine

HEARTS TOUCHED BY FIRE SERIES
The Wicked North, Book 1
Unconditional Surrender, Book 2
Rags & Hope, Book 3

STANDALONE READS
Her Eternal Rogue
The Wicked Bargain

Author Bio

A *USA TODAY* BESTSELLING AUTHOR, GINA Danna was born in St. Louis, Missouri, and has spent the better part of her life reading. History has always been her love and she spent numerous hours devouring historical romance stories, always dreaming of writing one of her own. After years of writing historical academic papers to achieve her undergraduate and graduate degrees in History, and then for museum programs and exhibits, she found the time to write her own historical romantic fiction novels.

Now, under the Texas sun and with the supervision of her three dogs, she writes amid a library of research books, with her only true break away is to spend time with her other life long dream – her Arabian horse – with him, her muse can play.

www.ginadanna.com
www.facebook.com/GinaDannaAuthor
www.twitter.com/GinaDanna1

Made in the USA
Columbia, SC
15 October 2021